SOMEONE

YOU

LOVE

IS

GONE

ALSO BY GURJINDER BASRAN

Everything Was Good-bye

SOMEONE
YOU
LOVE
IS
GONE

GURJINDER
BASRAN

VIKING

VIKING

an imprint of Penguin Canada, a division of Penguin Random House Canada Limited

Canada • USA • UK • Ireland • Australia • New Zealand • India • South Africa • China

First published 2017

www.penguinrandomhouse.ca

LIBRARY AND ARCHIVES CANADA CATALOGUING IN PUBLICATION

Basran, Gurjinder, author
Someone you love is gone / Gurjinder Basran.

Issued in print and electronic formats.
ISBN 978-0-7352-3342-3 (softcover).—ISBN 978-0-7352-3343-0 (ebook)

I. Title.

PS8603.A789S66 2017   C813'.6   C2017-900118-3
                                           C2017-900403-4

Cover design by Sarah Brody
Interior design by Terri Nimmo
Cover photograph by Shulevskyy Volodymyr/Shutterstock.com

Printed and bound in the United States of America

10 9 8 7 6 5 4 3 2 1

For Satvinder, Amit, and Arun—always.

This we have now
is not imagination.

This is not
grief or joy.

Not a judging state,
or an elation,
or sadness.

Those come and go.
This is the presence that doesn't.

RUMI

PART ONE

BEFORE

Amrita walked by his side and he by hers, two halves of a whole. When she was with him, a feeling rose up inside her. It wasn't until much later in life that she recognized it as hope.

NOW

I'm dressing for Mother's funeral, my back to the full-length mirror. No beauty but for what the poet might see, my child-bearing body scarred and stretched like a balloon blown up too many times. Two children. One dead now, dead from the start.

That baby. I imagine him buried, though he wasn't buried at all; he was burned. Incinerated. I never saw him, never named him. My mother said that perhaps it was best that the baby died deep in my womb, for what life could a child like that have? "One like Diwa's?" I asked. I expected her to reach over and slap me. But she didn't say anything, not a single word in defence of my brother and never a word for the dead baby.

Yet sometimes at night or just before dawn, I wonder if that baby died at all or if it crawled into my chest and ate my heart, tore it into small pieces and, over the past twenty-four years, digested it and replaced it with its dead body. A baby for a heart, curled into a fetal position, sucking its thumb, cold as a stone. And that feeling at the back of my throat, that sickening feeling that has grown since Mother died last week, was me trying to keep it all down.

A knock at the door. "Are you almost ready?"

"No." I sit on the bed, staring out the window, my white salwar puddled around my feet. Bare tree branches clawing at the open grey sky. Rain mists, and falls.

Raj comes in, closes the door behind him, and then stands there, surveying. I interpret the silence, a language we've coded and cracked countless times. "We have to get going. Everyone's waiting."

"There is no everyone." I stand up, pulling on the salwar, tightening the drawstring around my waist.

He glances at his watch. "We should have been there by now. The service is set to start in less than an hour." His sentences are like building blocks piled one on top of the other.

"I just need a minute."

Raj hands me a flask from his breast pocket and I take it from him, drawing out a whisky swig that closes my throat. This is the first real kindness he's shown me beyond our paper-like years of lists and tasks, letterhead and ledger items. I pass him the flask, his hand brushes mine, and for an instant I want to reach out, to draw him in and allow grief to transform into something else. But the moment passes and he tucks the flask away.

"I'll wait downstairs."

"Is she all right?" Sharon asks from behind the door.

"She's fine. She's almost ready."

"No, Dad, she's not fine. I'm coming in."

Sharon opens the door. "Can I help?"

She waits with the anticipation of a child wanting to be noticed. It's the same look she's always had. That pleading sort—see me, tell me I'm good, tell me I matter, hold my hand, tell me a story, make me feel needed. It was the same way with me and my mother, and it was no use.

"Give her a minute." Raj says this as if it's a warning.

"Okay, okay, relax already. I just thought she could use some support."

"I'm fine. I'll just be a few more minutes." I shut the door on Sharon's prying eyes. She's always seen through my layered emotions, tremors and quakes, our shared geology. I'm sure that's what drove her away. Raj insisted she wasn't leaving forever, that she was just choosing a university farther from home, but I knew there was no coming back. Every time she came home she was less as she was and more of who she was becoming.

From the window I watch Raj sneaking a cigarette, tapping ashes into the potted topiaries that flank the front door of our house. He paces the way he does when he's on an important call, only this time his pacing seems almost ridiculous. He looks older in his suit. His hair is white at the temples; he no longer has the mass to hold the cut of his jacket. It seems we are both less of ourselves these days. This is what I think of our life now. This is how I enter every new day: my daughter now grown, the years accumulating on the wrong side of the present. It's an effort. It's the feeling of walking though the desert, of looking for my homeland, the place of my ancestors, and knowing now that place and land are just things that bind us and hold us to ideas that don't exist. I want to tell Raj this. I want to say these things when the room goes quiet and we're in the deep pretending of life. The quiet turning of pages, flipping of channels, muttering of words.

I wrap myself in Mother's cream pashmina and look in the mirror. She stares back. Resemblances run deep in our family. Ancestors lay claim and features are passed on like antiquities, every new life an ode to another. I have her coal eyes, flecks of amber that spark when the light catches them at the right angle, or so Raj used to say in those long ago, up close, parted lip moments. I sigh and reach for my purse.

"We have to pick up Diwa on the way," I say, walking outside.

Raj nods. "We'd better get going then."

"How long is he staying at her house?" Sharon asks and hands me an umbrella, which I refuse.

"I'm not sure." I brace myself against the quick wind and hurry to the car, head down, avoiding her questions, not wanting to deal with the details of what happens after today.

"Is he going to live there?"

Raj glances at Sharon in the rearview mirror and starts the car.

"I told you, I'm not sure. We're just taking things day by day. What difference does it make?"

"I think it's odd."

"Well, it's his home too."

"I guess. I just think it would be strange now with Grandma gone. Doesn't he feel weird about being there?"

"How the hell should I know how he feels?" I say, my voice raised.

For a moment we sit quietly, listening to the windshield wipers groan and squawk. I look back at her. "I'm sorry. I shouldn't have yelled."

"Whatever." She stares out the side window, sullen-eyed.

"It's just been a hard day," I add, waiting for her to say it's okay, but she doesn't.

We drive the rest of the way to Mother's house in silence. I focus on the singular grey outside, willing it to wrap around me. Diwa is waiting at the end of the driveway. He's wearing one of Father's black suits. Mother gave it to him the day we were sorting through her closet. "I don't remember ever seeing Father in this," I said, pulling out a slender wool jacket.

"No, not that one," she said when I threw it on the donation pile. She asked Diwa to try it on and then measured the sleeve length, noting that it would need to be let out at least half an inch. "You look so much like him," she said, reaching up to adjust his lapel. Then she paused as if she'd lost her place in the moment. "Simran, drop this off at the tailor's for me, will you?" Later, when I picked it up, the tailor handed me a photograph. "This was tucked in the breast pocket," he explained. It was a black-and-white photo of Mother that I'd never seen before. The image was blurry, as if she'd moved just as the picture was taken and was caught in motion, in two places at once. Her hand was covering part of her face but I could still make out her profile, her shy smile that always made her look slightly embarrassed, the contours of her face, a single chandelier earring. She was young, younger and happier than I'd ever seen her. I tucked the photo in my wallet and have kept it there ever since.

Raj unlocks the car door and Diwa slides in next to Sharon. He says nothing, folding into our silence. He looks tired, worn through. Part of me wants to assume my role as big sister and assure him that it will be over soon, but I know that's not true. There is always something more.

The funeral is a small gathering. The casket is closed.

People assemble and collect, walk in single file, stoop-shouldered, unsure. Eye contact is fleeting and words are limited to small apologies. Clammy handshakes, tilted heads, pressed black attire. An old woman I don't know grabs my hands in hers and pulls me in. Her eyes are grey and clear. She says something but I don't hear her; I just look down at her feet. The scuffed shoes, the worn toe box, the flattened soles—it's as if she's been dragged kicking and screaming through her whole life. "Something pulls us through," Mother always said. The woman steps back, turns toward the magnolia-draped casket, then closes her eyes and says a prayer.

We sit tightly packed in the small front pew of the funeral chapel. My sister, Jyoti, sits across the aisle with her husband, Nikhil. Their two small children fidget in their starched, solemn clothes and speak in loud whispers that Jyoti quiets with a glance. I look away before she sees me staring at her, before there can be anything between us. I do that with everyone on this day, purposefully holding space and distance, fortifying walls and then drifting on the sound of prayers and personal reckoning. In my mind, Mother is ill and lying in her hospital bed. Tubes circulate fluids in and fluids out, her lips are parched, she's thirsty and I cannot give her water. She can't swallow. I tell her this, agonizing that I must deny her. She closes her eyes and I hold her paper-thin hands in mine. I marvel at them, resting in my palm like two white doves waiting to take flight.

Raj touches my arm. "It's time," he says as the prayer concludes.

Everyone stands. Jyoti crosses the aisle and embraces me, her head tucked into my shoulder, crying with an open mouth. "I can't watch," she says as the casket is moved. I tilt my head to see Diwa push the button that will begin the process of turning flesh and bone into ash. A few days ago, the funeral director explained the combustion process—the breakdown of body to gas and ash that takes several hours. He told us we were welcome to tour the facility if we liked; the cremation chambers were state of the art and reached up to two thousand degrees Fahrenheit. I declined his invitation and now I wish I hadn't. All I want is the intimate knowledge of what happens, of how it comes to be that nothing will be left. No physical proof of her wholeness.

After the funeral and temple prayers we return to Mother's house, where the remaining mourners gather for tea and consolation.

"These are the diehards," Sharon says, ducking into the kitchen, away from the living room full of women speaking in whispers. "Sorry, bad choice of words."

"It's fine. You're right." I put on another pot of tea.

She gathers her long hair and twists it above her head, tying it in a messy bun. "I don't know what they get out of it, coming here." She crouches down to look at her reflection in the chrome toaster and adjusts a wayward strand.

"It's tradition. This is how we mourn."

"Tradition or not, it's too much. When I die, I don't want any of it. All this crying. Grandma would hate it."

"Yes, she'd hate it, but she'd suffer it all the same."

Sharon stands up. "How does it look?" She's pointing to her bun.

"Lopsided," Jyoti answers as she comes into the room. "Here, let me." She starts fixing it. "Your hair is so thick, just like your mom's. You should get it thinned or layered or something. I'll give you the name of my stylist."

"That would be great," Sharon says, rolling her eyes when Jyoti looks away.

"Can you take the drinks out?" I pass them each a tray of refreshments, my hands shaking.

"Why don't you take a break, Mom. Maybe go lie down for a bit. We've got this."

I close my eyes and listen as they circle the living room, making polite offerings. The house is full and yet quiet; it's as if my ear is pressed against a wall, listening for some great truth. As if we're underwater, our lives submerged. I imagine the furniture dunking and bobbing, floating and sinking in the sea as we try to arrange it on the ocean floor, one hopeless piece at a time.

Jyoti comes back into the kitchen to refill her tray. "Seriously, you should go lie down; you don't look so good."

"You're right." I walk down the hall to the bedroom and sit on the edge of the bed. The room hasn't changed since I was a child. The two double beds covered in pink nylon bedspreads are separated by the only other piece of furniture, a clunky oak night table. Bare walls except for the religious calendars. Mother was furious when I took them down and rolled them up. "You can never turn your back on the Guru," she said.

"I'm not turning my back on anything, they're just stupid calendars."

"It doesn't matter. You cannot destroy the Guru's likeness."

"But what are you supposed to do with these when the year is over?"

She shrugged. "Some people have them cremated."

I laughed until I realized that she wasn't joking. "But that's dumb. Sikhs don't believe in idol worship, and these are just pictures."

"They are pictures that are staying on the walls," she said, tacking them back up.

Guru Nanak, Guru Gobind, Guru Teg Bahadur. I remember them all from the comic books Diwa and I found in the temple basement. How frightened we were when we read about the devotees being boiled alive and sawed in half. Even Guru Gobind's own children were entombed alive, bricked inside walls. When Diwa asked the Giani why this would happen, the priest sat taller and explained that Sikhs would rather die than abandon their faith. "There is honour in faith and duty," he told us. For weeks after that Diwa and I played Guru in the green space behind the temple. Wielding tree branches as kirpans, we fought the Muslims who came to convert us. When the Giani found out we'd been playing at God and casting other children as infidels, he told us that faith was not something to play at. But Jyoti never learned that lesson. Amid all this, these bedroom walls cloaked in religious pictures, Jyoti found Jesus. She was ten when her best friend, Christie, baptized her in their swimming pool and twelve when she started to attend church regularly. When I asked her how she managed to go to church without our parents knowing, she said there was nothing to manage: she'd tell them she was going to the library and they never questioned her. We don't talk much about religion anymore. She can keep her God and I can keep mine. That's what Mother used to say about it. Sometimes I dream of Jyoti enraptured. She sways and cries and falls before an altar, tears streaming from wide-open eyes. She has seen the light.

"You can't hide in here all day." I hear Mother's voice behind me.

"What?" I turn around and Sharon is standing in front of me. "What did you say?"

"Nothing," she says. "I just came to check on you. Are you okay?"

"I'm fine. I thought you were . . . I thought I heard . . ." I shake my head. "Never mind, I'll be out in a minute."

"Okay, take your time."

When she's out of earshot, I call to Mother. "Are you here?" I wait for a sign. I'm almost disappointed when none comes.

In the kitchen, dishes are stacked in haphazard piles all over the counter and the pot of tea is about to boil over. The milk froths over the sides as I pull it off the stove.

Sharon rushes in. "Sorry, I forgot to check on it." She reaches for a rag and starts to wipe up the spilled milk. "Here, let me," she says as I reach for a set of mugs.

I shoo her away, tired of her hovering. "No, it's fine. I've got it."

She stands next to me, unconvinced. "I can pour tea, you know."

"Fine." I step aside and let her overfill the china cups. When she's done I watch the tea lap up over the rims as I carry the tray to the mourners.

They weep and wail. They howl and burn their tongues on their tea and sympathy. How fragile and ugly it all seems.

After the last guests have left, I pull Raj aside.

"I'm going to stay the night. I don't want Diwa to be alone."

"What about Sharon?" he asks. "She's only here for a few more days before she heads back to school. I thought you'd want to spend some time with her."

"I do and I will."

"When?"

"I don't know. Do we have to figure this out now? I'm tired. I just need a day."

"She needs you, Sim. We need you. It's hard on us too."

"I know." I pause, wishing there was an easier way. "I just need some time to figure things out."

"It's been years, Sim. She was sick for years."

Numb, I don't answer. I can't even hear him.

I'm relieved when he stops talking and asking and waiting and wanting. He gives in and we surrender to the reality as we always do. Falling out of love. Aging. It all happened slowly and suddenly. His thinning hair, my thickening waistline, our busy schedules, distractions and preoccupations. I always thought I'd have more time, but now "It's too late" becomes a mantra. My thoughts are steeped in these probabilities, my humiliation and idealism stripped naked and left on display for my bitter aging self to feast on.

I watch him leave.

The house feels emptier without them. Without her. Her absence exists in things—her cane by the door, her walker tucked into a corner, her sensible shoes lined up neatly beside the stairs. She died slowly until the dying had a name and then it set in at full speed, one defeat after another. First it was her limbs, weighted down as if they were full of stones and twigs, swollen and aching at the same time. Her gait slowed, her foot dropping and then dragging in every misstep. She complained softly and at first insisted nothing was wrong. I took her to every doctor, every massage therapist, and every naturopath, until the specialists' diagnoses came and there was nothing to be done but wait. A terminal diagnosis that for some was almost immediate and for others was merciless and for her would be somewhere between the two. ALS. I memorized it in clinical terms. *Amyotrophic lateral sclerosis, the most common of all motor neuron diseases, is marked by muscle atrophy, fasciculations and spasticity, dysarthria, dysphagia, dyspnea. Wasting away of muscles, difficulty speaking, difficulty swallowing, difficulty breathing, the degeneration of upper and lower motor neurons.*

ALS. I memorized its origins and coded Latin roots. "A-myotrophic. No-muscle-nourishment." No muscle nourishment. I repeated it, whispering it at night when I couldn't sleep or when

I was washing dishes and caught my reflection, so much like hers, in the window. I wrapped my tongue around that first word, those five syllables. I slowed all three words down and pushed them from my lips, repeating them until I understood that there was no way out of those syllables, those coming events. I tried to imagine what it would be like and made adjustments to her home. I installed grab bars and rails, bought walking aids, and when that wasn't enough, I arranged for home care. But what I'd imagined was only part of it. Nothing prepared me for the moment when she went quiet, when she was confined to her bed and trapped in her body. When all she could do was look at me and all I could do was look away. I thanked God that Diwa was there for that moment, and for every one that came after it.

Diwa's in the kitchen making Ovaltine, mugs clattering, milk boiling. I watch his unchanged evening routine from the hallway. "You want some?" he asks without looking up. His hair has fallen forward as he leans over to pour the frothing milk into the mugs.

"Sure, but let me help; you must be tired from standing all day."

He leans against the counter and stretches his leg. "It's not so bad anymore, not like it used to be."

I sit at the table, forgetting myself for a moment as the past steps forward. The house is as it was before Father died, and even before that, before Diwa left and before Jyoti was born. It had a different light then, or perhaps that's just memory casting a glow, candlelight and sunset, everything only slightly visible. Mother is in the kitchen, washing the dinner dishes. Steam is rising and the window in front of her fogs over her reflection. Even here, she is a ghost. Father's in the living room listening to the hockey game on the portable radio and Diwa and I are playing in the attic. It's 1977. He is three years old and already remembering. In another three years he'll be sent away and Jyoti will be born to replace him. I take the glass mug of Ovaltine from him and wonder what he still remembers, if the doctors left him with anything besides scars and silence.

"You remember how we used to play under this table?" Diwa asks as he sits down next to me.

"I remember how we used to *hide* under the table."

"He wasn't all bad."

"No, I don't suppose he was."

"How he was—it wasn't his fault, not really. Before Mother died she told me he was sorry for everything that had happened."

"Aren't we all?"

I pause as the clocks from Mother's collection sound the hour. From every room come staggered chimes, cuckoos calling out. A moment later, the sound of ticking. The house a metronome. We are empty, as if our insides have been carved out. That is what death does, I think. It makes us into ticking clocks, in need of winding, hollow and mechanized.

"It was a nice service," Diwa says. "Simple. She would have approved."

I smile and sigh. "It's strange. Being here and her not being here."

"It is."

"I wonder if it will get easier."

"It doesn't get easier, you just get used to it." Diwa sips his milk.

My head droops, wilting like a flower. "I'm sorry. That was insensitive of me. I should have thought, I mean, I . . ."

"It's okay. Those years, it wasn't your fault. We don't need to talk about it."

"Do you *want* to talk about it?"

He shakes his head. "No, not really."

"Another time?" I'm hopeful.

"I don't see the point." He gets up from the table, the chair legs screeching against the linoleum. I watch him walk to the sink and rinse his mug. He washes it out and lays it on the drying rack. "I think I'll turn in," he says.

"It's been a long day. I should do the same."

After he leaves I sit with my eyes closed for a few minutes before I get up from the table.

"I'll wash and you dry?" Mother says. At the sound of her voice I drop the mug and it shatters into pieces at my feet. "Always clumsy, just like your father," she says and kneels down to pick up the pieces. "And a good cup too . . . what was the occasion?"

I stare at her for a moment. She's solid. Not a ghost. "You can't be here."

She looks up. "And why can't I be? I live here."

"Are you okay?" Diwa calls from down the hall. "I thought I heard something fall."

Mother places her index finger against her lips and raises her eyebrows.

"It's fine. I just dropped something," I yell back. "I've got it. You go to bed."

"You sure?"

"Yeah. Goodnight." I hear him shut the door. Mother smiles.

"This isn't real," I say, shaking my head. "You're not real. You're dead." I begin to collect the shards of glass in my palm.

"Real, not real. What does it matter?"

"But you're dead," I say again, dropping the glass into the garbage can.

"I'm fine," she says. "See?"

I turn to see. She's gone, nothing but broken glass in her place. My heart drops into the task of picking up the pieces.

THEN

Diwa writes poetry. Mostly haikus. He taps each of the seventeen syllables with his pencil, numbers them on the rungs of his fingers, searching for physical ways to count. He scribbles each line on a strip of paper he's cut to match the fortune cookie message he's kept in his pocket ever since our neighbour, Mrs. Shum, gave him the treat.

He has thousands of blank slips of paper in his dresser drawer and jams at least ten in his pocket every day, just in case. He never knows when a poem will come to him; he told me that he feels them coming the same way animals feel a storm approaching. He feels the words swirling in the distance, travelling through space and time, until finally they thunder down from the sky. Sometimes he catches only a word or maybe a line, and most often he leaves a trail of papers along the floor, never picking them up when the poem is complete, never revealing the whole to anyone, not even me. His printing is tight, the letters crowding each other like a row of bad teeth, painful and apologetic all at once. Sometimes I try to make sense of them, but usually I can't be bothered with my little brother's weirdness and let his trail go cold. Mother picks up the slips when she tidies the house before Father comes home.

It's the only time she picks up after us; I help her with it and other chores. When she was dusting yesterday she stopped suddenly and said, "In India, we had servants who did this."

"Why don't we have servants here?"

"Ask your father."

It took Father's stinging reply on my rear end for me to realize that she didn't really mean for me to ask him. She was just talking in opposites the way she does. She felt pretty bad about the spanking and said I didn't have to do my after-school chores today. Most kids would be happy about that but I hate the mess. I make sure all of Diwa's toys are put away in their colour-coded boxes.

As I sort the cars from the blocks, Mother looks over at me and says I'm like Father that way. "So picky. Everything always in order."

Diwa dive-bombs onto the couch. "Order in the court, speak up, monkey, now!" he shouts. He points at me, zipping his lip, invoking our quiet contest. He stares at me, making funny faces, and when that doesn't work he tackles and sits on me, his metal leg brace digging into my thigh. He tickles me until I break into laughter. "You're a monkey! You're a monkey! I win!" he says, jumping up and down, his papers falling out of his pockets.

"You're the monkey," Mother says. "See what a mess you've made!" She swats him off the couch and he rushes to the other room, plopping in front of the TV to watch his cartoons. Mother collects the slips and puts them in her cardigan pocket, never reading them until after dinner, when the house is quiet. I've wondered what she finds there, in all those scraps she can't part with. She doesn't throw them out the way she throws out the arts and crafts I make at school. She collects his poems, storing them in Mason jars and tucking them in the kitchen cupboard, just behind the dented canned goods. Once, when I was playing Harriet the Spy, I opened those jars. Every word smelled like strawberry jam—every phrase like a scratch 'n' sniff sticker. Mother keeps most things in jars, so it isn't a surprise that she keeps his scraps of poetry there. There are jars of buttons, candles, cake decorations, foreign coins, pennies, and pencil stubs all over the house. What others see as junk interests her; she takes great pains to collect what was once useful and could be useful again. On neighbourhood spring-cleaning days she pilfers through the piles of household items and small appliances that people leave out. She fills Diwa's little red wagon with an assortment of tools and collectibles and pulls it home, the rear wheel squeaking and veering in the other direction.

It was during one of those trips that she realized she could also collect pop bottles and beer cans and return them for the deposit. After spending an afternoon in front of an adding machine figuring how much pocket money she could make, she hitched the wagon to Diwa's bike. Each week she hunts through the large bins behind the mini mall, looking for plastic, tin, and glass, and then Diwa pedals them all home so that I can sort them. Mother says that the pedalling is good for Diwa; it will strengthen his weak leg. He might not even need to wear his brace for much longer.

For the dollar she gives me I don't mind sorting through the glass and cans, but I'm glad I don't have to ride around the neighbourhood with her. The kids at school make fun of the Punjab and the retard who take the cans. Diwa isn't really retarded, or mentally disabled, or handicapped, or slow, or any combination of the words people use when someone is different, but he is different. Even the doctor said so. When he told Mother and Father that Diwa was "a special case," Mother was relieved but Father muttered, "The boy is special all right, a special idiot." The doctor paused and then kept talking about Diwa's IQ as though he didn't hear. I realized then that people do this when they don't know how to respond. They do this a lot when it comes to Diwa. "But what about the things he says?" Father asked. "That's not normal." He looked at Mother, who was pleading with him, her face a web of concern.

"Simran, take your brother outside." She handed me his vinyl backpack filled with Hot Wheels cars, as always dismissing me just when things were getting interesting. In the waiting room, Diwa crawled beneath the bank of plastic chairs and lay tummy down, tucked out of sight, lining up cars with his usual precision. I wondered what the doctor was talking about and stood in the hall, straining to listen, but all I heard was the muffled talk of other patients in other rooms. Nurses in their white skirts, stockings, and sensible shoes walked by with clipboards, looking at me with the same washed-out eyes and smelling of the same kind of clean—perfume, nicotine, and bleach. One scent covering another. I breathed it in as they passed. It made me feel a part of something.

Mother and Father didn't speak of what the doctor said.

They barely speak at all now. Father stops off at the pub each night, comes home late, beer on his breath, and sits in front of the TV eating his dinner, watching whatever is on. Every night he falls asleep during the nightly news and startles, bolting up like a scared animal, when a commercial comes on. Always with the same sleepy-eyed question: "What, what time is it?"

"It's okay, Papa, just rest. You're tired." I pat him on his balding head. He reaches for my hand and kisses it. He loves it when I call him Papa instead of Father.

"Such a good girl," he says. "Such a nice daughter."

The only bonus to their not talking is that in his half-drunk, half-asleep time I can ask him for anything.

"Can I sleep over at Janie's house?"

"Yes, of course. Janie, she's a nice girl. Good family," he says, his breath blowing warm and lazy on my face.

"Can I have a dollar to go to the candy store?"

"What? Candy? Sure."

"Can I wear my hair down for picture day like the other kids?"

"Yes, tell your mother it's okay."

Sometimes, when he's snoring, I put a newspaper on his lap and slide his reading glasses down the bridge of his nose so that he looks like the dad on *Father Knows Best*.

Once the cleaning is done, Mother moves to the kitchen to peel carrots for the subzi. Diwa has gone off to his room to play, leaving the TV on full blast again. "I'll turn it off," I say, so that she knows it was Diwa who left it on. But he won't get in trouble the way I would because he's her baby. Last week I got yelled at for giving him gum, even though he was the one who'd left it all chewed up and smushed into the shag carpet. Mother made me pull out the taffy-like pieces with tweezers. She doesn't even seem to notice that Diwa's acting stranger than usual, spending more time in his room muttering to himself. I try to get him to snap out of it, but it doesn't always work and sometimes he gets angry and punches me. Last week he knocked out one of my baby teeth. I put it under my pillow, hoping the tooth fairy would make a stop at our house just this one time, but every morning the tooth was still there. Mother threw it out, saying that there was no such thing as the tooth fairy.

I lean back into Father's recliner and pretend I'm in a rocket ship, ready for takeoff. I press imaginary buttons and count down. Before I get to one, Mother shouts at me from the kitchen. "Simran, go check on your brother."

"Do I have to?" I yell, bolting the chair back upright.

"Simran!"

"Okay, okay."

Diwa is sitting on his bedroom floor, staring at nothing, the way he's been doing since the doctor gave him new medicine.

"Want to play?" I hold out a set of jacks in the palm of my hand. He doesn't look up.

"I'll let you go first."

He still doesn't answer, so I pull his favourite dinosaur puzzle from the shelf and set it down in front of him. I sit cross-legged on the green shag carpet. "How about a puzzle? I'll let you do the corners."

He tosses the puzzle aside and the box spills open. Pieces scatter across his bedroom floor.

"Now look what you've done," I say, collecting the pieces. "If you keep this up, I'm going to tell Father."

"He's not my father and you're not my sister."

I roll my eyes. "That's right, how could I forget."

"You weren't even born yet. You don't know anything."

"Riiight," I say, elongating the word the way the popular kids at school do when I tell them stories about Diwa's episodes. Episodes—that's what Mother says the doctors call his remembering.

"No! Wrong. You can't say 'right' because you weren't there."

"Okay, okay. Please calm down before you get us both in trouble."

"I won't calm down." Diwa is up on his feet now, yelling.

"I'm sorry. I didn't mean it," I say, hurrying an apology before Mother hears us and comes shouting up the stairs with a wooden spoon in hand.

"You're not sorry. You're a liar."

I take him by the shoulders and look him square in the eyes. "Really, I'm sorry." I keep hold of him until I see his eyes soften.

"Swear it?"

"Swear it. Cross my heart and hope to die." I mime an *x* on my chest.

"Stick a needle in your eye?"

I nod. "If I lie, I die."

He waits for a sign. "Okay," he says finally. "I'm not mad. You can be my sister this time."

We shake on it, even though, as so often before, I have no idea what he's talking about. Half the time he doesn't even sound like himself, saying things that no one understands except Mother—and even then whatever he says makes her cry. When he has big fits only Mother can console him. Father doesn't even try. All he does is yell from his armchair, "See, you see . . . that's not normal. That's not special," and then the sound of another beer can opening.

Every family has routines, and this is mine. I tell myself that at school when Jennifer, the popular girl, talks about her Avon mother with the feathered hair, her Wayne Gretzky wannabe brother, their family's Disney vacation. I tell myself that she has her routine and I have mine. It's just different. It's just special. Special like Diwa.

NOW

I wake to an emptiness and lie in bed, listening to the house sounds—creaking bones, cracking knuckles, the aches of staying in the same place forever and slowly sinking into it. Above me the spackled ceiling is cracked, signs of a shifting foundation. I sit up, reach across to the window, and lift a slat in the blinds. It's raining. I put on my slippers and pad across the hall to my mother's room. I take in the loneliness of such utility—a hospital bed, a night table, a dresser with a bouquet of wilted roses. In the end stages we cleared her room of everything but the essentials. Her replica Queen Anne bedroom set was moved to the basement spare room and all her possessions were packed and moved out of her wheelchair's path. At the time I thought it was the right thing to do—it would help keep her here as long as possible—but now I'm not so sure. I shut the door and move on down the hallway. The walls are cluttered with grade-school pictures and faded 8 x 10 Sears portraits of the people we used to be, naive in our secondhand clothes and stupid grins, the colours muted by time.

"Diwa, are you there?" I ask before entering his room. His bed has been made and his slippers lined up at its edge. There are three stacks of papers on his desk, each with a small stone placed on top. I try to read his handwriting; it's all loops and tangles, like a spool of thread unravelling on a page. He's writing poetry again. When I sit down on his twin bed, the metal frame squeaks and the mattress sags and buckles. The sound takes me back to Diwa's night terrors—the sound of him waking up in the middle of the night and then Mother rushing in to comfort him. I'd stand at the door and listen to her telling him he was all right. "I'm here," she'd say. I can hear her now if I try, and how I do try.

My phone rings. The number registers as "home." I don't answer it.

By the time I return, Raj has left for work and the house has the feeling of recent abandon. The scent of coffee and aftershave linger, outlining his morning rush. The paper is splayed on the kitchen table with the crumbs of his half-eaten toast scattered over the headlines. I pick it up and toss it in the recycling bin. "Mom?" Sharon calls from the other room. She always calls out in query when there's something to be said, something on her mind.

"Yes, in the kitchen." She comes in, her backpack hanging off one shoulder and her suitcase dragging behind her. "You're leaving?"

"Yeah, I think it's best." She drops her backpack and leans into the doorway, her face half hidden by her layers of wavy hair. The light is hitting her from behind and she's all aglow, her face obscured until she steps forward. She has Raj's sharp nose and thin lips, a face full of intention.

"Your dad said you might stay for a bit."

"Yeah. It's just with exams and everything I think I should get back." Her voice rises, lifting on the last word as if she's asking a question. I hate it when she intonates this way, no comfort in the completeness of a phrase. It's as if she's always asking for permission.

"I wish you'd stay, just for a few days."

"Well, it doesn't seem like you really need me here." She tosses her hair away from her face. "You weren't even home last night."

"I know, I'm sorry about that. I just needed some time." I try to hold her gaze but she's moved on, her eyes fixed on her cell phone. I stare out the window, watching the leaves drop. "It's complicated."

"Tell that to Dad. I feel sorry for him," she says while texting. "He doesn't know how to help and for that matter neither do I." She puts her phone in her jeans pocket.

"I didn't realize you felt that way. I thought you understood."

"I do." She sighs. "It's just, I don't know what I'm supposed to do. I think it would be better if I go and then you can take all the time you need."

"So, you've decided already. Nothing I can do."

"Like I said, I have exams." She crosses her arms over her chest. I know what comes next: she expects the back and forth of *please stay* and *don't go*, of wanting to be needed and my not wanting to need. The idea exhausts me.

I nod and tighten my lips. "Okay then, I guess I'll get my keys and drop you off at the ferry terminal."

"Don't bother. Ryan's picking me up." Her arms are still crossed. "He just texted; he's outside."

"Oh, I didn't realize he was in town."

"Um, yeah, he came with me. For moral support."

"Moral support? Funny, I didn't see him at the funeral."

"I told him he didn't have to come. Family only and all that."
She looks down at her feet and tosses her hair again, avoiding my
disapproval. "Oh, and by the way, the flowers, umm, from the
funeral, I didn't know where to put them so I just left them in the
garage. I wasn't sure what you wanted to do with them."

"The flowers? No, that's fine. I'll sort it out."

Her phone pings. "That's probably him. I should go. We're
trying to get the two o'clock sailing." She slings her backpack
over her shoulder. "Mom, you're going to be okay, right?"

"Me? Yes, of course . . . it's just going to take some time."

"Dad told me to tell you that he'd be home early this afternoon. He needed to go in and wrap up a few things. Maybe the
two of you should go away for a couple of days. You know, a
change of scenery?"

"Maybe. I'll have to think about that. There's still so much to
do." I walk her to the front door, unable to come up with the usual
litany of warnings and parental advice. "Do you have everything?"

"Yes."

I move in to hug her but she's already pulling away and my arm
hooks her in an uneven embrace. I lean against the door and watch
her walk to the street, where Ryan is waiting in his beat-up, hand-
me-down Saab. He embraces her and then places her bags in the
trunk. Their bodies lean into each other as they rearrange the cargo,
moving bags, making room. They touch each other without effort or
thought, and for a moment I remember that feeling of easy love.
That feeling when Raj and I were first dating, the anticipation of
each other, the act of exploration and discovery; it was part of every

breath, and my life had meaning and beauty because of it. The feeling tightens and hardens in my chest before settling back inside me. Sharon waves one more time before getting in the car, and in a moment she's gone. I don't blink, I don't exhale, I don't move until the car has turned the corner. My heart drains. In my mind, my daughter, seven years old and weeping, stares at me from the back window of the summer-camp bus. She hadn't wanted to go, but Raj insisted; even when I told him how upset she was, he said it would be good for her. That evening I couldn't stop seeing her tear-stained face, so much like I imagined Diwa's when he was sent away. Telling Raj I had to visit my parents, I drove the three hours to the lake to bring her home. I expected to find her alone and forlorn but there she was, sitting around a campfire with all the other children, telling ghost stories with a flashlight to her chin. I backed away slowly, with the caution of someone walking away from a wild animal. I got back into my car and drove home before Raj realized where I'd really gone, before he could tell me he'd been right and my worry had been for nothing. I never explained that it was me who wasn't fine, that it was me who had to retreat from seeing her existing without me. She didn't need my reassurance anymore. She didn't need anything.

"Just space and time—that's what young people need," Mother said during those troubling teenage years. "And both are just an illusion." I never understood her meaning, until now.

"Time and space." I repeat this as I tidy the house, read my emails, and retrieve the twenty-eight voicemail messages that have been waiting since Mother died. All sympathy and sorrys, except for the one archived message from Mother. "Simran, it's me. I need your help with something. Call me back."

I sit cross-legged on the floor, holding the phone in my lap and listening to the message on speaker a dozen times before saving it. I never knew what she wanted help with. I hadn't called her back.

"So ask me now," Mother says. I turn around; she's sitting on the sofa behind me, knitting. "What? Don't look so surprised to see me. Go ahead and ask me, will you?"

"Mother, what did you need?"

"Help with the TV remote control."

"Mother, what did you need?"

"Someone to talk to."

"Mother, what did you need?"

No answer. She's gone. Again.

I sit in her silence before wandering to the garage to take stock of the flowers. I hadn't planned on buying so many. Mother would have considered it a waste of money. But after I'd walked through the showroom of silk-lined caskets and was in the chaplain's office, looking through laminated photos of themed floral arrangements, I couldn't stop myself. "Only the best will do." I plunked down my credit card to buy the last gift I could give her. Eventually I settled on the Serenity series—yellow roses, white magnolias, ivory orchids, hearty gladiolas, and delicate freesia all arranged in extravagant wreaths and sprays that flanked the mahogany casket and lined the walls of the chapel. Thousands of dollars. Raj didn't say anything when he saw the bill. He doesn't say anything now as he pulls his car into the garage and sees me sitting on a cheap plastic patio chair among the wilting remains. I've been sitting here for over an hour. I get up slowly, stretching my back, and as the garage door lowers again I'm suddenly aware of the stench of dying flowers.

"I don't know what to do with them," I say. "What do people do with them?"

He shuts the car door and surveys the scene. I recognize the look on his face. Sympathy and patience. He's good in a crisis.

"I'm not really sure." He sidesteps the wreath. "Did you ask the people at the funeral home? Maybe they can be donated or something."

"Maybe."

I pluck some freesia from a bouquet and offer it to him. He puts down his briefcase. I tuck it into his lapel and stay there for a minute, leaning forward, my head close but not touching his chest. He reaches for me, his hand in my hair, his breath on my neck.

"It'll be okay," he says.

I step away. "I know."

A moment passes. "When did you get home?"

"Just a few hours ago."

He nods.

"Sharon left."

"I know. She told me she was going to leave early. I think it's all been a bit much for her."

"I suppose. I was just hoping she could have stayed longer. There's so much to think about."

"Jyoti and Diwa can help," he says. "And, of course, I'm here. Let's talk about it when I get back."

"Get back?"

"I've got to run out and meet a client for drinks. I'm sorry, it's obviously terrible timing, but I can't postpone it . . . I'm sorry. I just came home to change. I should be back by seven at the latest."

"Of course, I understand, you go. You have important things

to do and I—I'm just . . ." I pause, not knowing how to say what I want, what I need.

"Sim, it's not like that and you know it."

"What is it like, then?" I watch him struggle with what to say. "How could you possibly know? You still have both your parents."

He looks away, ashamed or annoyed, I'm not sure.

"All I know is that I'm stuck in the middle of all this, and for everyone else it's over," I say.

He reaches for my hand and I pull it away. "It's not over, you're right. And it's not fair that I have to go to this meeting, but that doesn't change the fact that I need to go."

"If you say so."

"Look, why don't we have a late dinner tonight? We can talk then." He has a wilted smile, the kind that's lopsided and apologetic. So easily forgivable.

He kisses me on the forehead and then disappears into the house, only to reappear a half-hour later, showered, clean, and new. He is wholly perfect and I'm still in yesterday's funeral clothes. I can't tell if the reek is the dead flowers or me. I haven't showered in days.

"Okay, I have to go. The cab's waiting out front. I didn't want to drive."

"Good call." I try not to be suspicious. Unlike me, he's never warranted it.

"I'll see you later."

After he leaves I stare at the sagging stalks of gladiolas, the shrivelling blooms, and am overcome with the cloying smell of what I can only describe as "after." I open the garage door and close my eyes, inhaling slowly. I gather buckets and vases from around the house, fill them with an inch or two of water, and bring them into the garage one by one. Then, with scissors in hand, I slowly pluck single flowers from the wreaths and sprays, clipping and salvaging what I can. I place the stems in water and then tear at the foliage—pulling the ferns, twigs, and leaves from the floral foam and laying them out on the worktable, assessing. I gather up twine and ribbon and bind the flowers together in a hundred miniature bouquets and corsages, the first of which I place on my husband's windshield.

I fold down the backseats of my SUV and set the bouquets in rows, piling them one on top of another. Then I drive to the strip mall where Mother used to buy her groceries. For a time I watch people getting in and out of cars, unloading their Walmart carts, and I rethink my plan. I glance back at the banks of flowers, recalling how they draped and flanked the casket. I wish I'd burned them and let them turn to ash like everything else.

I start with the back lot first, working my way in and out of the parked cars, placing one bouquet on each windshield. No one seems to notice me until I'm on the last row. A security guard watches curiously before approaching. He is young and heavyset, the sort of boy who should play rugby. "Ma'am, you can't be doing that."

"Doing what?" I move to the next car.

"Whatever you're doing there with the flowers."

I look up. "What? It's illegal to give away flowers?"

He says nothing and I continue.

"It's private property, ma'am. I'm going to have to ask you to stop."

I keep going. "Look, I'm almost done here. Just a few more to go."

He stands in front of me, his hand on his hip as if he's reaching for a gun, but it's only a radio. He calls for backup. "Ma'am, I'm going to ask you nicely one more time. Please stop what you're doing."

When I don't stop he reaches out and grabs my arm which makes me drop the last bunches. I kneel down, picking them up quickly and pressing them to my chest. "Look what you've done. You ruined them."

"Ma'am, I'm sorry, but I warned you."

"*Warned* me?" I stand so close to him that he has to back up. "You warned me. Jesus Christ, they're flowers. For fuck's sake, *they're just flowers!*" Another security guard emerges from the store, yelling at me to calm down. As a crowd forms I shake my head and start to laugh at the ridiculousness of it all. "They're just flowers. You know, no one tells you what to do with them." I throw the remaining bouquets in the air.

Then I back away from the scene, stepping on a few of the roses as I head back to the car. As soon as I pull the door shut I rest my head against the steering wheel, wondering what to do next. My phone rings, Mother's number on the display. I want to believe that it's her, that she saw what just happened, that she sees she's left me alone and that I don't know how to be alone. I don't answer the phone. Instead I start the car, and as I do, the security guard approaches. I roll down the window. "Now what?"

He leans into the open window, his face close to mine. He has blue eyes and a constellation of freckles on his nose.

"Ma'am, are you all right? Can we call someone for you?"

I can't help smiling when I tell him no.

He steps back and I drive away. I keep driving into the twilight, past the city, toward the quiet of mountains, forest, and water. Mother is with me, sitting in the passenger seat.

"You are driving too fast."

"I'm doing the limit."

"Too fast, but then you always were in a hurry, weren't you?"

"Fine. I'll slow down." I glance at her. She isn't sick anymore. She's wearing her finest clothes, the coat with the fur trim, gold earrings.

"Where are you going?" she asks.

"To the park."

"It's not the same anymore."

"I know."

"You won't find what you're looking for."

"I know."

"The answers you're looking for—they aren't there."

"I know. But tell me, where should I go then?"

No answer. I look over. She's gone.

I park at an abandoned campsite where my parents brought us as children for weekend trips. Mother was right. It's been overtaken, the earth reclaiming itself in moss and fern, the old clearings covered in forest brush. Accompanied by a deep and watchful silence, I wander through the dark woods, stumbling over knotted roots and meandering on and off the trail toward the break in the trees. Nightscape surrounds—crickets, the occasional hoot of an owl, the sound of my own breath—until finally I reach the lake and collapse on the cold ground. The sky and moon reflect a mirror image in the glassy water. I lie on my back and let the night sky bend around me. I pull it close, counting stars until they dissolve into dreams. I'm ten and tiptoeing through the forest in my flannel nightie toward Diwa, who's lying on the beach with his red toy telescope. I lie next to him and we stare up at the constellations.

Diwa: "How many stars are there?"

Me: "I'm not sure, why don't you count them."

Diwa counts, whispering numbers toward an infinity: "There are too many."

Mother whispers: "As many stars as there are lifetimes." She nudges me awake.

It's still dark and my body is damp and weary from the cold. I get up and check the time. I've slept for hours, and though it seems like only minutes, it's enough. I collect myself and drive toward the city lights of home.

Raj is waiting in the darkened living room. "Where have you been?" He turns on a lamp and the room lights up in shades of sepia.

I hang up my coat in the hall closet. "I went for a drive."

"And this," he says, holding up the bouquet I left on his windshield. "What the hell?"

"I don't know." I slump down on the couch. "I'm just tired."

"I got a call from our neighbor. She saw you at Walmart, loitering in the parking lot, leafleting the flowers on cars."

I chuckle. "I guess we can't shop there anymore."

"It's not funny, Simran." He pauses, struggling to find a compassionate tone. "It's been a lot lately. Your mom, the hospital, the funeral . . . all of it. You need to get some help."

"I don't need help. I just need some time."

"You of all people know that time isn't enough. Remember after the baby. You were a wreck when—"

"Don't even," I say, cutting him off. "This is not like that and I can't believe you'd even bring it up."

37

"I'm sorry. I just mean—I don't want to lose you again. You should call someone, or I can call someone and make an appointment for you. It did help last time."

"That was completely different. Trust me, I'm not depressed. I don't need help."

"Sim, you need someone to talk to."

"That's why I have you." I'm smiling, trying to take the edge off.

"Then talk to me. Tell me what's going on." He leans in closer.

"I don't know what you want me to say."

"It's not about what I want, it's about what you want."

"What I want is to not talk."

"That's exactly what I mean. It's why you need a professional."

"Fine, go ahead, make the appointment."

"That's it?"

"That's what? You should be happy—I've just agreed. What more did you want?"

"I want you to tell me why you'd do this, the flowers, all of it. And where have you been? Why didn't you call me? I was worried."

"I just wanted the flowers gone." I walk over to the bar cart, pour two glasses of Scotch, and hand him one. "I wanted it to be over. But it's not." I clink his glass and down my drink.

BEFORE

The flowers for the wedding—clusters of foxtail orchids, jasmine, and magnolias strung in garlands. Orange, red, and ivory place settings, gold accents and linens, silver lights strung through the village trees, a canopy of light. None of it would come to be. What Amrita imagined was just a dream.

THEN

"The cane was a gift," Mother says while making room in the attic for boxes of Christmas ornaments and porcelain nativity pieces she bought at a garage sale. "Please put it back where you found it," she adds, restacking boxes. "It's not a toy."

"Why would someone give you a cane?" I twirl it in my hands like Charlie Chaplin and walk the attic's perimeter, ducking about the eaves and gables so I don't bump my head.

"It wasn't a gift to me. It was a gift from me."

Diwa grabs the cane. "It's mine. She gave it to me." I yank it away from him and he teeters and falls. All the attention diverts to his scraped knee and the bruise that will eventually form. He cries the way he always does, big and awful. His mouth wide, streams of tears and mucus.

"Stop being a baby."

"Simran," Mother says, reprimanding me with a look. She

reaches for Diwa, quieting him in an embrace. "There, see—you're okay, you're fine."

He snatches the cane from me, sticking his tongue out. Then he stands up and stares at the foreign lettering on the handle, running his fingers over it as though he's deciphering Braille. He reads it out loud:

In life after life, in age after age, forever.

Mother's eyes are wide. "How did you read that? Who told you what it said?"

He looks at her and says matter-of-factly, "It's mine. You made it for me."

She kneels down and stares at Diwa as if she's looking deep inside him. "Who told you to say such a thing?" Her eyes are full of wonder and horror. She shakes him when he doesn't answer. "Who told you?"

"You're hurting him," I say, trying to loosen her grip.

Diwa is calm and insistent. "You did, Amrita. You gave it to me. Don't you remember?" He pulls away from her grasp. "You gave it to me before you married Manohor." He puts down the cane, sits on the wooden floor, and lines up his cars the way he always does.

Mother gazes at him with disbelief.

"What's he talking about?" I ask. "Is this another episode?"

"Be quiet, Simran," Mother says. She sits down next to Diwa. "Is this what you remember?"

Diwa's attention is fixed on winding up his toy car. He watches with delight as it unwinds, shooting across the floorboards. He gets up to retrieve it.

Mother grabs his hand. "Is that what you remember from before?" she asks again.

"Yes, I already told you. Manohor was my brother when I was called Pyara." He shakes off her hand and runs to grab his car, making engine noises as he drives it across the floor.

Mother's eyes well up. She gets agitated when he says things like that; these things make her nervous, make her go quiet and blank in the eyes. She tries again. "Diwa, you know Father doesn't like it when you speak like this. Who told you to say these things?"

Diwa looks up and smiles. "No one. Remember, it's like that poem you used to like . . . it goes:

> *I died as mineral and became plant,*
> *I died as plant and rose to animal,*
> *I died as animal and was a man.*
> *Why should I fear? When was I less by dying?*

"Where did you learn that?"

"I don't know. I just remember it."

"What else do you remember?"

"I don't know." He shrugs and packs the cars inside the carrying case that Father bought him for his birthday. "I'm going to watch *Scooby-Doo*," he announces, and then rushes down the stairs and turns on the television. I can picture him sitting right up close to the screen again, disco-ball eyes mirroring light.

"You'll go blind if you sit that close," I holler, leaning over the stair railing.

"Okay, okay." He turns the volume up.

Mother hasn't moved. She's still sitting on the floor.

"Are you all right?" I ask.

She nods, her body shuddering. She's crying soundlessly.

"Shall I make you some tea or can I get you some water?" This is all I know to offer. For Father it's beer, for Mother it's tea.

I ask again, and this time she says yes in a half voice, looking up with some small gratitude. "Simran, don't tell your father about this. Please." She reaches for my arm and I help her down the narrow stairs to her room.

She wipes her eyes as if she's wiping cobwebs from corners. "He mustn't know." She waits for confirmation.

"I promise. I'll never tell anyone." I'm really not sure what I've promised or what any of it even means, but I like the quiet of a secret, how it makes me feel special. "What about the doctor—shall we tell him about this episode?"

"No, the doctor won't understand."

I don't understand either. I've been writing down clues in my diary, trying to piece things together, but none of it makes sense. "Mother, did Father even have a brother?"

"Yes, he did. But he died a long time ago."

"Oh." I don't know what else to say, and I can tell Mother doesn't want to talk any more, so I go to the kitchen to make the tea. While the water boils I pull out my diary and open the latch. With the matching pencil, I jot down the date and the incident. I lick the tip of the pencil the way old-time detectives do on TV and underline the words *cane* and *dead brother*. Diwa shouts from the living room that he wants juice.

"Okay, in a minute." I finish my notes before pouring him a glass. "Be careful. Don't spill," I say, handing it to him. He doesn't look away from his cartoons. "Pyara! I said be careful." He still doesn't answer and I'm relieved that he's just a little liar after all.

"Don't worry, he's just playing make-believe," I say when I give Mother her tea. "It's all in his head."

Mother is propped up in bed like a stuffed doll. Her eyes are distant, staring into space, focused on solving a puzzle, a riddle, an equation. She takes a sip. "Remember what I said: not a word to your father."

I shut the door so that Mother can rest before Father comes home. Then I pick up after Diwa, who's fallen asleep in front of the TV. Mother hasn't sent him to school this week because his medicine makes him groggy. I turn the TV off and put a blanket over him. He looks peaceful and happy, like a small animal at my feet, all curled up and purring.

When Father comes home the house reanimates as if there were never a silent secret afternoon. Mother makes roti while I get Father his beer and turn on the CBC newscast. He doesn't comment much on anything he sees, except for the occasional *tsk* from the corner of his mouth. He's quiet most days after work and likes to just recline in his La-Z-Boy chair. Mother says that driving a taxi is hard work, but I don't think she really means it because of how big she makes the words sound.

"Simran, come and set the table," she yells.

After I set the glassware out, I ladle the daal and subzi into the silver taals, careful that the lentils and vegetables stay in their tin compartments. If different foods touch each other, Diwa will refuse his meal. We eat our dinner in silence. Father doesn't like to talk; he complains that people in his taxis talk non-stop and that he hates the idle chatter. "Silence is a virtue," he often says. He chews with his mouth open, shovelling in forkfuls then washing them down with gulps of water. He wipes the water off his chin with his sleeves, first one and then the other. Then he looks at Diwa, who hasn't eaten anything. "Something wrong with your food?"

"No," Diwa answers, stirring his daal clockwise then counterclockwise.

"Well, are you going to eat it or just play with it?"

Diwa pauses as if he's actually deciding.

"He had a big lunch today," I say, lying for him.

"He can be excused then." Father breaks off a piece of roti and sweeps it across the taal, catching the last lentils.

Diwa jumps down from his chair and wanders off to his room.

"He has an appointment tomorrow," Mother says.

"What appointment?" Father's mouth is full.

"With the new doctor, remember? You said you'd take us."

Father doesn't look up. "No, no. I'm working tomorrow, I can't go."

Mother motions to me to clear the table. "If you won't go, how will I get there?"

"You're so educated, I'm sure you can figure it out." Father tilts his head in mockery.

"You know I don't know how," she says, looking away.

"Take the bus. Simran can go with you." He turns to me. "Right, Simran? You can help your mother."

"She has to go to school," Mother says before I can answer.

"If the appointment is so important to you, she can miss one day."

"It should be important to you. *You* can miss one day."

"I told you the last time." Father is looking straight at Mother now. "I'm not going to any more of these appointments. All the damn tests. You know as well as I do that none of it will help. Besides, the last doctor gave us medicine for him. What more does he need?"

"The medicine is no good. You see what it does to him. Is that what you want? Half the time he just sits there."

"That's better than before, isn't it?"

They exchange long looks of quiet contempt. "So, you want to know what happened at school today?" I ask, trying to change the subject. Neither of them looks at me; it's as if what I've just said has dissolved and I'm invisible.

"You won't go with me. Fine. Have it your way." Mother collects the taals, dropping them in a clattering pile in the sink. Father retreats to the TV. They don't speak for the rest of the evening. Diwa and I stay in our rooms, avoiding the tripwire of their silence.

The following day, I miss school to go to the doctor's with Mother and Diwa. I don't mind so much—I get to sleep until the bell would normally ring, and while all the other kids are doing their multiplication tables I'm taking three bus transfers to the city and then an elevator to the twentieth floor. I stare out the tinted window to the street below. "It's true what they say: everyone looks like ants."

Mother hushes me. Something about waiting rooms and public spaces puts her on guard. She wouldn't even talk on the bus. When the lady at reception beckons to us we follow her to a room that looks more like a library than a doctor's office. "Wow," I say, taking in the expansive wall-to-wall bookcases. "What kind of doctor is this?"

"A book doctor," Diwa says, twirling the globe that sits on the antique desk before rushing to the floor-to-ceiling windows. He presses his whole body against the glass.

"Diwa, stop that. Come sit down," Mother calls. He jumps on the leather sofa before she grabs him and holds him tight. She whispers warnings in his ear and he relaxes. I sit down next to them on a black chair across from the big desk, pulling out the clipboard and notepad I brought with me. I've written the date and the doctor's name and underlined them twice.

When he comes in he says hello, and unlike other doctors, he shakes Mother's hand. "You must be Diwa," he says. Diwa dips his head and curls into Mother's lap. The doctor sits at the desk and thumbs through a file. "Mrs. Am-reeta San . . . doo," he reads. He looks over his glasses at Mother to make sure he's said the name correctly. Then he says it again, this time with more authority. "Mrs. Sandhu, you were referred to me by your family physician."

I translate and Mother nods impatiently. She understands most things, but says white people speak so quickly that she can't find her English words fast enough to reply.

"Today is a preliminary discussion on how we can help Diwa. But before we can start that, why don't you tell me, in your own words, why you're here."

"How do you spell pre-lim-inary?" I ask him, scribbling my notes as quickly as I can. "So I can look it up later and tell Mother what it means."

He looks at me as if he hadn't realized I was in the room. "It means the first of many appointments."

I jot it down. "Got it."

I can't tell if he's annoyed or intrigued by me. Now that I'm ten and a half I'm too old to be cute and am more like a stick insect—skinny legs, knotty bones, big teeth. I try to translate for Mother but she's already parroting in her broken English. She doesn't understand.

"It says here," the doctor continues, pointing to his chart, "that Diwa has had some delusions. Can you tell me about them?"

Mother is shaking her head.

"He thinks he's someone else," I say for her.

"Is this true?" he asks Diwa.

Diwa doesn't answer.

"What's your name, son?"

"Diwa," he says.

The doctor smiles and says it's common for children his age to make things up.

"It's true," I say. "He makes things up all the time. Last week he said he was Superman and wouldn't answer us unless we called him Clark Kent."

"No, not made up," Mother says and implores me to explain that Diwa remembers things sometimes.

I sigh and roll my eyeballs. "A few times he's said his name is Pyara. But Pyara is my father's dead brother so he really can't be someone who's dead, right?"

"How often has he believed he's someone else?" the doctor asks and then writes something down.

"I don't know, just a couple of times. But sometimes he gets really mad."

"If that's the case, Mrs. Sandhu, I would like to see Diwa alone for one-on-one counselling and behavioural tests."

"Tests, what tests? He already had so many." Mother is flustered.

I calm her down and then, after referring to my notes, I tell the doctor that Diwa has already had eight appointments with our family doctor. "My mother wants to know why Diwa needs more tests."

"Not medical tests," he says, looking at Mother. "Diwa needs to be observed by specialists. He needs counselling."

"Specialists," Mothers repeats.

"Yes, we have some of the best doctors working out of the hospital's psychiatric ward. His case is quite unique."

I explain this to Mother, who is shaking her head. "He's not crazy."

"Mrs. Sandhu, that's not what we are suggesting here. We want to help your son, but he does need to be admitted for observation, even just for a day."

"No," she says.

The doctor sighs and tries again. I can tell he's frustrated because he's speaking louder. "It says here that your son has been violent, that he's punched his sister and has even hit you when you challenged his delusion."

I translate and Mother says, "That was only one time. All children fight. He's just . . ." She stops and searches for the word. "He's hyper."

"I understand that this is upsetting." Mother looks away and the doctor lowers his voice. "Your son is very special. He has some unique talents and abilities, especially in written language, yet these delusions seem to be holding him back from exhibiting all the traits a healthy six-year-old would. We need to understand why this is. The file mentions that Diwa was premature and oxygen-deprived at birth. Is that true? If so, we should assess if there have been any developmental delays."

"Oxygen depri . . . ?"

I can't think of how to translate this, so I remind my mother of the cord around Diwa's neck when he was born, but she's still unsure, speaking in rapid questions, statements, rocket fire and blame. I explain it again, and this time out of frustration I reach for the doctor's phone and hold the cord up near my neck for effect. Mother slaps my hand away. I'm ashamed of the charade, but it was the only way I could think to describe it.

I was there when Diwa was born. When he came out of Mother quiet and blue. We were on vacation in India, staying with our great-grandmother. It was Diwali night. Father had gone to see the festivities, but I wasn't allowed and so was watching the fireworks from the window, delighting at the explosions of light and sparks fading into the night sky. Everything was alive. Except for Diwa. Mother had gone into labour early, and only an hour later Dadi ji summoned me from the window, instructing me to run and get the lady named Pasho who had delivered half the children in the village.

When we first arrived, Pasho had put her hands on Mother's swollen belly and said, "You again." Mother nodded that yes, she had returned home. Pasho smiled at her for a long time. Now I was knocking on her door. No one answered, so I ran through streets and gullies shouting her name until she appeared. I didn't need to say anything. She already knew.

By the time we made our way back, Mother was screaming and Dadi ji was pulling the baby out of her womb, slick with birth and blood. I stood there, stunned. The floor was awash with fluids and waste. Pasho pushed Dadi ji aside. The cord was tangled around the baby, wound around his throat, tied up in his legs and arms. He looked like a slippery fish caught in a net. Pasho unwrapped the cord, hooked her finger into the baby's mouth, and laid him down, her mouth on his, breathing life into him. Mother was wailing, Dadi ji was praying, and Father was outside banging on the door, demanding to know what was happening. I opened the door and he charged in, standing frozen in the middle of the room amid the carnage of birth. His shadow loomed on the walls that had been decorated for Diwali—candles in clay pots lined the windows. It took less than a minute for Pasho to bring the baby back from death, to bring him back from darkness.

The doctor is still talking about the importance of one-to-one observation and psychiatric counselling. I try to catch up to translate but by now I'm lost. I've even stopped taking notes. Mother is withdrawn, seemingly assaulted and offended by all the doctor has said. He writes a new prescription and hands it to her. "We'll try this for now. But I'd like to see Diwa again. Please discuss it with your husband." She nods and we all walk out of the office, defeated. In the elevator, we watch the numbers go down. "It's okay," Diwa says, taking her hand.

The three of us sit side by side and ride the bus in silence. Thankfully, Diwa falls asleep; I can look out the window undisturbed. I watch the houses, buildings, and trees go by in a blur. Everything looks like part of the next thing. The streets bend and meander, change names and change back again. There are corner stores and big stores, there are cars and trucks, there are one-way roads and highways. We speed past farms and low-lying fields, greenhouses, hothouses, through cities and suburbs and across the bridge. From the bridge I can see the on-ramps and off-ramps, the rivers and mountains—and the separation of this place and that place disappears. I realize that every road and every place and every person is just a way home.

A cool breeze sweeps the mustard fields and the koel birds swoop and pitch, flying from tree to tree. Amrita is lying on the veranda swing when she hears him whistling, his voice carrying across the lush valley, the land of five rivers. Home. Occasionally he sings a few lines of "Likhe Jo Khat Tujhe," and she hums along with his velvety voice. She saw *Kanyadaan* at the cinema before she came home from girls' college and can't stop singing the songs. She spent the last week of exams imagining a love like the one Shashi Kapoor sang of—where love letters become flowers and stars.

She closes her eyes, listening to his voice, falling into that same daydream. The sound draws closer and then stops. He's leaning against the neem tree, taking a long, slow drink of water. He wipes his mouth with his hand, puts the canteen back in his satchel, and walks toward her. She sits up, taking him in. He doesn't wear a turban like the other men in the village, and his black hair is cut short like a foreigner's. He looks like a man in a film—smooth olive skin, wire-rim spectacles, a clean, pressed white shirt, the leather satchel stuffed with rolls of paper and ledger books. A natural perfection about him. "You like that song?" he asks.

She quickly glances behind her to see whether the servants have seen him talking, but they're busy in the kitchen preparing lunch.

"I heard you humming," he says.

When she realizes that she's smiling and looking right at him, she averts her eyes.

"You are Sardar's daughter? Amrita?" he asks, daring to use her name.

She doesn't answer.

"The villagers say you've just returned home from school."

She nods, economizing words and gestures. "And who are you?"

"My name is Pyara, miss. I work for your father."

"What do you do?"

"Irrigation schematics, miss." He pats the satchel.

"You are the engineer Father has mentioned?"

"Yes." He wipes his brow, and she watches the remaining trickle of sweat slide down the side of his face. A flutter moves through her chest. Something takes hold in her throat; her mouth is dry. She looks away and back again.

"My father has known your father for many years. Since Pakistan," he says.

"Since Partition?" She is longing to talk about something important. Since she's been home from school there has been only the non-stop chatter of her cousin's upcoming wedding.

"He has not spoken of us?"

She tilts her head from side to side, a maybe yes, a maybe no.

"Our families travelled together during Partition, through the riots."

"My father, he doesn't speak of it—because of my mother," she says.

"Nor mine," he says. Amrita suspects he's lying. She's heard everyone but her father talk about it. Her mother went missing during a night raid. She was found the next day, face down in a paddy field, her torso slit open from end to end. Her father was so distraught that he had to be carried away from the scene, but overnight his despondence turned to vengeance. He vowed to kill two Muslims for every dead Sikh. And so it went on all sides, Muslims and Sikhs massacring each other. Death for death, the toll of a division never fully realized until it was too late. She's read the statistics and horrid details in her history classes. Tens of thousands were kidnapped, raped, and murdered during the largest forced migration the world had ever known. Amrita's mother was just one of them.

"I was only a child then. I don't know much about it," she says, perpetuating his lie.

"Nor I."

Again, she wonders if he's lying. Millions of people moved across the new borders. Caravans of children and women on ox carts, men walking with all their possessions on their backs. "I've overheard the servants talking about the marauders, the violence, the hunger, and disease. It must have been terrifying." She says this before realizing that she's speaking too much for a woman. In so many ways, she is as her father's mother, Dadi ji, said she was— an impudent child. While other girls her age learned the trade of a woman, she was sent to school. She was taught how to speak some English, to say words like *please* and *thank you*. Words that had no ready equivalent in Punjabi.

She assesses the distance between them. Only a few steps. She's never been so close to a man without a chaperone. She wasn't even allowed to come home on the train by herself. "I am told it is a blessing that I don't remember. That I have no stories," she says.

"Isn't all of life a story?"

She smiles and again looks away.

"Amrita," her grandmother calls from inside the house.

"Yes, Dadi ji!" she yells and stands up quickly, looking back at the house. "My father is in the study. You mustn't keep him waiting."

Dadi ji is in the front room, her eyes fixed on her embroidery. She looks up over her glasses when Amrita sits in the chair across from her. "I was calling. Where were you?"

"Just outside, resting."

"Resting," she scoffs and continues her needlepoint. "How much rest do you need? You've been home for four days and you haven't even unpacked your trunk. Every time I go to your room there it is, in the corner, as if you've just arrived. I should have one of the servants unpack it for you."

"No need, I'll do it." Amrita leans forward to look at Dadi ji's handiwork. "What are you embroidering?"

"Linens. A wedding gift for your cousin." Dadi ji holds it up for Amrita to see. "Come sit here and I will teach you how to do it."

Amrita sits next to her on the settee and watches as Dadi ji works the needle through various stitches. Dadi ji hands her the hoop and the needle. "You try now."

She runs the needle through the fabric. She cannot even master the most basic running stitch, and within a moment has pricked her finger.

Frustrated, Dadi ji takes it from her. "Here, let me show you again." She runs the stitch back and forth several times and then hands it back to Amrita.

After thirty minutes and several failed attempts, Amrita hands the needle back to Dadi ji. "I'm afraid I'm just not very good at this."

Dadi ji undoes Amrita's uneven stitches. "Well, it's not your fault. Your father should have let me teach you these things long ago, but instead he sent you to school as if you were a boy. First boarding school and then girls' college, filling your head with all kinds of ideas instead of practical skills. You don't even know how to cook. Who will marry a girl who cannot cook?"

"I'm not getting married yet."

"Not yet, but soon enough, child."

"Well, I'm sure you can teach me, or maybe one of the servants?" Just then the cook comes in to tell Dadi ji that lunch is almost ready.

"The servants have their own work to do. No time to teach you such things. I don't know what my son was thinking. I warned him, you know. I said too much education for women is a bad thing . . . leave the schooling to men and the child-rearing to women. That's how it's always been and that's how it should be."

Amrita stands up and crosses the room, staring out the window at the empty swing as Dadi ji drones on. She watches Pyara cross the courtyard of their gated compound and leave through the same gate where she first saw him. "Dadi ji, who is the boy Father has hired?" Amrita sits down casually.

Always suspicious, Dadi ji squints at her for a long time before answering. "He is home from London." She looks back down at her needlework. "He completed his studies and has returned to help his family, but soon he'll be going abroad. His brother will stay and take care of the farm."

Amrita smiles and whispers his name under her breath.

Dadi ji drops her cross-stitch and stands up. She leans over Amrita and pulls her ear, twisting it ever so slightly. "Did you hear me, child? I said he is leaving."

"Yes, I heard you," she says, flinching until Dadi ji lets go of her ear.

Now Amrita vaguely remembers having seen him and his brother before. As children they used to play in the fields behind her house; she would watch them from the balcony. His twin brother, Manohor, was Pyara's shadow, tailing him from sunrise to sundown, yet his smile was only half as wide as his brother's. It seemed unfair that the qualities of their halves were so unequally divided.

NOW

I'm waiting in the therapist's office, already clutching the throw pillow that's been casually placed on the couch. I've unwrapped and eaten two hard caramels from the candy dish, bracing for yet another session without a defined outcome. First I'll unburden myself. Then I'll have to confront my sense of having no purpose—and that lack, that void, will be the centre of every session until I reach acceptance, which I'm told is somehow different from settling. Acceptance in therapy is like enlightenment in spirituality: virtually unattainable. I wonder how I can speed up the process, get more quickly to the moving on, to the being all right with the business of everyday life. I should know how to do it. People die all the time. Everyone goes through this. I'm trying to steel myself against the hardened reality of death and grief and the tunnel it bores through me, a black hole, universes collapsing inside. I try not to think. Every thought made real is like a landmine. So here I am, three times a week, blasting myself to bits. Raj will ask me how the session went. I'll tell him that it was good, that it helps, but I hate him for asking, for inserting himself into the cause of remaking me into something he only remembers. I look around the small windowless room. The lights are dim, the plants are fake, the vanilla from the scented candle wafts and circles. I'm clamping down on another caramel, cracking it in two, when Marcia, the therapist, walks in.

"Sorry I'm late." Marcia sits down, pulling out her notes from my last visit. I'm reminded again that she looks too young to be a therapist. How can a twenty-something strawberry blonde who bounces when she walks have any real advice, any real experience of the world? Life must be easy for her. She probably wears those horn-rimmed glasses just to look smarter. After barely scanning the notes, she asks me how I'm doing. She's smiling and overly cheerful for my liking. Doesn't she remember that my mother is dead?

"Dead? I'm not dead, I'm right here," Mother says. She's sitting next to me, handbag in her lap, looking unimpressed. "But I don't know why you thought to bring me here."

I block her out and focus on Marcia. "I'm good. A bit better, I think." I know how to get through the hour. I'll say enough to make her feel as though we're getting somewhere. I'll knit myself into half-truths, stitch together lies and facts until even I can't tell which is which.

She looks at me over her glasses and puts the notes aside. I saw the white coats do this with Diwa a hundred times. They'd put the notes away so that it would look as if they were paying attention, that they were talking person to person, not doctor to patient or clinician to subject. But everything that made Diwa special was marked as symptoms or postscripts on some chart. The white coats took what observations they could, prescribed pills, and left us all to live inside a heap of hopes and fears. But I don't tell Marcia this. She'd think I was crazy for believing that my brother is my dead uncle. Just thinking it sounds mad.

"Good for you. Don't tell her about Diwa. She won't understand you, just as they never understood him," Mother says, her arms crossed. Now she's standing over Marcia's shoulder, reading her notes, shaking her head. "All these doctors are the same."

"She's not a doctor," I accidentally say out loud.

"Who's not a doctor?" Marcia asks.

"What, no. Nothing, I was just thinking. Sorry."

"You would have been a good doctor," Mother says, looking at the framed certificates on the wall. "You should have stayed in school or at the very least gone back after the baby. That poor baby. You were so sad. We couldn't get you out of bed for months, remember? Back in my day the nurses called it the baby blues, but your generation, you have to give things fancy names—postpartum depression. No wonder you didn't get out of bed. And look, here you are again, letting them tell you you're depressed when you're just sad that I'm gone."

I ignore her, hoping she'll go away and let me concentrate.

Marcia looks down at her notepad and then back at me again. "So you said you're doing better. That's great to hear. Tell me more about that."

"More about how I'm doing, you mean?"

She nods.

"You're paying this lady to ask you how you are?" Mother sighs. "You should keep busy. You'll feel better if you're busy. That's what I told you after that baby and that's what I'm telling you now."

I try to orient myself. "Okay. Well, Raj is busy at work and that's fine. Sharon's still at school studying finance. She's like her father that way—economics interests her, so she's happy."

"But what about you? Have you thought about going back to work? It's been several weeks now."

I pause, taking stock of the time that's passed since Mother died. Each day stretches into the next. I've tried, but I don't seem to be able to carry on the way I expected to. The five stages of grief seem to have collapsed in on themselves. I'm debilitated but I won't admit this, especially not to Marcia, especially when I've lied about everything else. She still thinks I'm a doctor, that I have the life I'd set out to have. "Work, no. I don't think I'm ready to go back."

"What makes you say that?"

"Just the idea of seeing patients. It doesn't appeal to me. I mean, I want to help people, but . . ." I pause again, backing away from the truth. How could I have helped anyone when I could never even help myself? I clear my throat. "It's just that the clinic can be tiring."

"The clinic," Mother scoffs. "Of course you're tired of it—working as a nurse, never meeting your true potential."

"Sometimes routines can help with the grieving process," Marcia says.

"By 'help' you mean speed it up, right?"

"Oh, I see. You want to forget me already?" Mother puts in.

"No, not speed it up. Just help provide purpose or a rhythm of sorts."

"I don't know. I can't see that happening."

"That's right. You tell her. You need time to grieve," Mother urges me.

"And what would feel better for you?"

I hug the pillow and close my eyes for effect. "I guess I just want something else. Something more."

"That's always been your problem, Simran. You want too much," Mother says.

"Well, maybe not something more. Something different." At this point I'm not sure who I'm answering.

Marcia's eyes light up and she leans forward. "And do you know what that is? What you want?"

"No. I don't, not really."

She waits, forcing me to speak, forcing me to fill the silence with some introspection.

"I just want things to matter again. I want to believe that there's a point and a purpose to all this." I wait for Mother to chime in. But she's gone. My thoughts, unaccompanied now, drip in my head like water in a tin can.

"Do you feel purposeless?"

"I don't know, maybe." I've heard friends wrestle with this mid-life crisis, this pervasive lack of meaning; the chasm is as real for me as it's been for them. Everything seems different. Even Raj. With Mother gone and Sharon at university, it seems that I have no need for him, that the two of us have outlived our life together. I've seen it happen to other couples. The fights and reconciliations repeating until they pull up the very roots of the marriage. Declarations like "We don't want the same things" and "We're already leading separate lives" have become commonplace coffeehouse talk, brunch fodder for the girls. But for me it was different: there came a moment when I didn't love him. It wasn't the way people usually describe it—it wasn't a drifting apart, a backward distancing, it was simply a break. I don't remember what we'd been fighting about, but I do remember the feeling.

Kill or be killed. At the height of our argument he said he'd learned to hate me, that I was "a cold and selfish, cynical aging bitch." That fatal blow ripped through my chest. I felt the blood vessels bursting and blooming in my face, the sound of my own body so loud that I couldn't hear him anymore. The next morning he apologized, tried to act as if it didn't matter. He made coffee, talked about his day, sighed in defence, and pretended. He pretended and I pretended along with him. I gave him that but nothing else.

For a moment, I forget that Marcia's waiting for me to elaborate. "What would give you purpose?" she asks, persisting in the theme. She's a cognitive behavioural therapist, not a real doctor. She probably got her degree online or at a community college. I'm tired of this charade and shake my head. She moves on. "How are things with your brother and sister?"

"My sister? Same. She and I don't talk much. Now that my mother's gone, there isn't much of a point in trying."

"Why's that?"

"She's different. That's all I mean."

"How so?"

"She's really religious and well, I'm not."

Marcia makes a note. "Why does that bother you?"

"I wouldn't say it bothers me. I just don't understand the need for it. Don't get me wrong, it's fine to believe in God, but for her that's all there is. Nothing and no one else matters."

"Do you feel you don't matter to her?"

I grimace. "I'm not sure. To be honest, I just don't get it."

"Many people find comfort and acceptance in faith. For many it answers the question of purpose that you were speaking of earlier," she says, circling back.

"Touché," I say, impressed that she connected the dots. "I guess religion—well, it's just not for me."

"Were you ever close with your sister?"

"No, she's a lot younger than me. I wasn't really part of her life."

"And your brother?"

"My brother? He's fine. He's still living at my mother's house. I suppose he'll stay there or, I don't know, maybe we'll sell it." I think of Diwa—hunched over his writing desk, standing at the kitchen window watching the chickadees on the bird feeder—and smile at the simple comfort of his company. "He's doing well. He's not exactly how I remember him."

"How do you remember him?"

"I don't know." I hate that I say "I don't know" so frequently now, but death has taken all my certainty, has left me flailing. "I don't really remember him per se. I suppose I remember more how he changed things."

"And how's that? What did he change?"

I think back, images cycling through my mind. The day he was born, hiding under the table, playing in the attic, catching poems, pulling the red wagon, the doctors, the hospital. The stories Mother told me when she was dying come into focus, offer clues and make everything clear. She's given it all a meaning I can't share. "He changed everything."

I leave the session tired. But instead of going home I drive to the beach and then wander along the shoreline, picking up stones and casting them into the ocean. I want to stay there, meandering along the edges of land and sea, remaining in the between. The in-between is where Mother must have lived her life after Diwa remembered, after Father forgot, after everyone was gone and before she asked me to make her life whole again and bring Diwa home. I inhale. There's an autumn breeze that carries the scent of rain and burning leaves, the smouldering of a season. I think of what I didn't tell the therapist, all the things that haunt. I've reached the fat middle of my life and it's devouring me. Eating away at me in small details, feeding on me when I'm sleeping, anxious and dreaming, always asking what's next, what's next. And although my life is overflowing, glutinous in its haves, I'm ravenous. It's at these moments of hunger and discontent, this gnawing question mark, that I'm willing to forget everything I've ever known for something honest and real. Full Stop.

Full Stop. Like in a telegram.

Clicks and code, delineating ends and beginnings.

Hello. Full Stop.

The sound of an opening door. The sound of an opening heart. The sound of here we go, here I am. Imagine if it was enough.

Full Stop.

I think of it as starting with a telegram, although it was actually a phone call in the middle of the night. Mother's own full stop. News of Pyara's accident. She never parted with all the details, but she did tell me how the colour drained from her face, how fear surged through her body. She had so many questions. And yet her father never answered, preferring to shepherd his own version of the truth. He would always do what was best for her even if she didn't know it. "It was 1968," she told me. "Fathers were different then, daughters were different then. You did as you were told. You didn't think whether you liked it or not." Her regrets were few. If she'd had them at all, she didn't share them with me. I was her daughter and she was my mother: boundaries and distinctions that I felt each time we spoke. I interpreted it as distance. Mother interpreted it as perspective. She's standing next to me now, her salwar hitched at the knees, water lapping at her ankles. "It's cold," she says, laughing as she skirts away from the tide. "Aren't you cold? You should be wearing a sweater under that jacket."

I watch her walking, letting her take the lead as I trail a few feet behind.

"Why so sad, Simran?" she asks without looking back.

"Because you're gone."

"Gone, not gone. That's not it." She turns to me.

"What do you mean?" I'm frustrated with her riddles.

"You were always sad, always mad."

"That's not true."

"Isn't it?" She picks up a stone and casts it into the water. "Can you remember a time when you were happy? Really happy?"

"Yes, of course I can."

"When?" She's still throwing stones.

"Seriously, you want me to give you a specific example?"

"Sure." She pitches another stone in, watching it skip. "Look at that!" She smiles, congratulating herself. "Look at all those ripples."

I stand next to her, watching them spread and disappear into themselves. I watch as the water settles and think of how quickly the disturbance is forgotten, how quickly the ripples become the whole. For a moment I imagine filling my pockets with stones and sand and walking into the water—until I too am part of the whole.

THEN

I stand at the window pelted with rain, waiting for Father to pick me up in his taxi so that I don't have to walk to school in the storm. Outside the trees are swaying, littering the street with evergreen boughs and broken branches. I zip up my coat and rush down the stairs when I see him pull in. "Wait, Simran," Mother calls, hobbling down after me with a thermos of tea. "For your father," she says, out of breath. Her face is swollen, just like the rest of her. The baby is overdue. Last week Mother had pains and went to the hospital, but it wasn't time yet. The doctor says it could be any day now. She hands me the thermos. "Do you have your lunch?"

"Uh-huh." I grab my book bag. She hugs me but I try to pull away. "I have to go. I'm gonna be late." My body is squished up against her stone-hard abdomen. Ever since I saw her stomach at the hospital, the red and purple stretch marks—as if the baby were tearing and clawing its way out—I've avoided all contact.

Besides, she started hugging me only after Diwa left. "You're all I have now," she said, crying, even though it wasn't true. Father says the hormones make her crazy. They argue all the time, and when they aren't arguing she's either sleeping or crying. He says it's because of the pregnancy but I know it's because Diwa is gone. "I gotta go," I say again and lunge for the door, slamming it on my way out. I sit in the backseat of the taxi. "Hello. To Hawthorne Elementary, please," I say, pretending I'm a fare. I see Father smile in the rearview mirror and pass him the thermos of tea.

"Just a minute, ma'am. Coffee break." He pours the tea into a steel mug, takes a sip, and spits it out. "Goddamn it," he shouts. He rolls the window down and dumps out the tea.

"What's the matter?"

"Nothing," he says, shaking his head.

"Was it too hot? Did you burn yourself?"

"No, no. It's fine. Seatbelt on?"

"Yes, sir," I say, smiling. He puts the lid back on the thermos, drapes his arm around the back of the passenger headrest, and reverses out. The windshield wipers screech against the glass. "Did she use salt instead of sugar again?"

"You know your mother. Baby brain makes her crazy."

I nod, even though I know she did it on purpose. Last week she laundered his white button-down shirts with the colours. "You know what they called me at work today?" he asked her, pointing to his now pink shirt.

"How should I know?"

"Pinky. Goddamn it."

Mother hid her laughter, but I saw it in her eyes and I'm sure Father did too. She is a master at degrading him in small yet meaningful ways.

He doesn't say much about these slights, but when he has some liquor in him, he tells her what a disappointment she is. Last week he said, "Yes, dear. You are too smart for me, so educated, so wealthy, too smart to be a wife . . . I should write to your father and tell him what happens when women are treated like men." He lurched forward with a beer in his hand. "I'll tell him that these women, they think they can piss standing up. But instead they just piss all over you."

"This from a man who spits when he speaks and staggers in drunk every day," she said as he teetered toward her.

But I understood what he meant. Mother was the first woman from her village to have a degree, the first woman to have prospects outside the home. She wasn't trained to be a housewife. When they first moved to Canada it was Father who taught her how to make rotis, daals, subzis. It was Father who taught her how to buy groceries, how to chop onions and vegetables, and it was Father who asked the landlord's wife to teach her how to do the washing, how to operate the machines. Mother told me she hated the "fat, dark, buck-toothed wife of the alcoholic pig" they rented a room from. "That woman lorded her domestic uselessness over me. She thought she was better than me." But Mother was a good student in all things, and over the course of that year—the year they lived in the backroom addition of the decrepit city house— she learned how to do the things one must do to survive. Food. Shelter. "The most basic of Maslow's hierarchy of needs," she said. Father, who came to Canada with just a high school equivalent, found work driving a taxi. Mother said he could only ever aspire to more of the same. And when she'd complain of how far their life had fallen, he'd remind her that they had no choice in the matter. "No choice," he'd repeat for effect. Sometimes I try to imagine Mother living and sleeping in one-room squalor—a small cot, her belongings crammed into one bureau drawer, a house with no electricity, plagued by roof rats and cockroaches. She said it was worse than what any of her servants had ever endured. I try to picture her, how she might have been at the front of a lecture hall, her hand high in the air, answering the professor's questions on Sufi poetry, but I can't quite get there; the details are out of focus. Her life before I was born is an idea that has no edges.

"Almost there," Father says, turning onto my school's street.

"What was Mother like when she was in school?"

"I don't know. I didn't know her then. Why don't you ask her?"

I'd never do that—remembering makes her sad. Occasionally I see flashes of her; fragments of stories come into view and I see how she was once so much more. "Life just takes it out of you," I've heard her say many times. I used to wonder why she was so cruel to Father, and for a time I tried to protect him from her attacks. But now that he's sent Diwa away, and he's left me alone, and he's replacing one child with another, I realize that Mother is paying him back for a lifetime.

"Just let me out here," I say, motioning to the drop-off zone. He pulls the car over and I slide out, saying goodbye as I slam the door shut. Then I walk, head down, toward the office to give the principal Mother's note.

"It's in your handwriting," Mrs. Dean says, holding up the page.

"I wrote it for her. She signed the bottom." I point to Mother's scribbled name.

Mrs. Dean pushes up her glasses, rereads the note, and then takes them off, letting them dangle from the golden chain around her neck. The windows are fogged up and the room smells of coffee and paper. "Your mother didn't say when we can expect your brother to return to school?"

"No, we aren't sure how long he'll be in the hospital."

"Did they say what's wrong with him?"

I shrug. Mother told me not to tell people about his remembering. She still called it "remembering" even though the doctors had different names for it.

"All right then. Off to class, before the bell rings." She dismisses me with an upturned chin.

I head down the hallway, past the single-file lines of primary kids, to my classroom. Mrs. Carlisle is waiting at the door. "Good morning," she says in a sunny voice that makes everything sound like rainbows and surprises.

"Good morning, Mrs. Carlisle." Her blue eyes brighten. She has permed red hair and drives a sports car. All the kids like her, and so do I. She never yells; she always just asks you to do your best.

"Hey, Simran, is your brother still at the crazy hospital?" Peter asks as I hang my coat in the cloakroom. He nudges his sidekick and then repeats himself, making a show of it. "What, didn't you hear me? Are you deaf or are you crazy too?" His friends burst into laughter and make cuckoo gestures, twirling their fingers around their ears. My face turns red, and the tips of my ears are on fire. I swallow hard.

"That's enough, boys," Mrs. Carlisle says. "Don't make me say it again. Get to your desks and take out your readers."

She ushers us into the classroom, and like sheep we herd in for the day's lessons.

———

When I get home Mother is bent over, breathing heavily; her face is flushed, her teeth clenched, her eyes closed. Between breaths, she tells me to call Father.

Unlike Diwa, Jyoti is born in the safety of a hospital. By the time Father and I are allowed to see her she's been wrapped in a pink blanket and placed in the nursery with all the other babies. The maternity ward is decorated in pastels, the waiting rooms stocked with comfortable chairs, magazines, coffee stations. While I'm waiting I wander into the gift shop with its helium "It's a boy!" and "It's a girl!" balloons in the window. I thumb through the greeting cards, then turn to the wall of stuffed animals and pick up a teddy bear. "Can I help you?" the cashier says from the counter.

I put the teddy bear down. "No, thank you. I'm just looking. I have a new sister."

The cashier nods and goes back to her *People* magazine. I walk out along the corridor lined with pictures of storks, one for each baby born. Here, birth is a joyful event; all the labouring and warring is done behind closed doors, away from watchful eyes and listening ears. Here, they hide how one thing becomes another. When Father calls to me I follow him through a set of double doors and down the hall to where they keep the babies. I stare through the window that looks onto the nursery and ask Father, "Which one is ours?"

He taps the glass and points to the one baby who isn't crying. Her eyes are shut tight; to me she looks like a skinned kitten. Father isn't happy—he wanted a boy, a reason to never think of Diwa again. But as I look through the glass at my new sister, all I can think is that someone is probably looking at Diwa through glass right now.

The doctors at the hospital watched him through a one-way mirror, making notes, asking Mother and me the occasional question. "Does he usually grab at the air like that?"

"Yes, he's catching poems," I explained.

"Poems?"

"Yes, he writes poems."

"Interesting. Have you seen them?"

I nodded. "Mostly haikus. He likes the structure. He likes to count the sounds."

"That's interesting. I'd like to read them." The white coat made notes. "It's interesting that he can write at his age."

"I taught him," I said. "He's a fast learner. Even his teacher was surprised."

"Interesting."

I counted how many times he said *interesting* and wondered why he found everything about Diwa so absorbing. Couldn't he find something or someone else to study?

"And his walk? How long has he walked like that?"

I watched Diwa. Step, shuffle, hop. Step, shuffle, hop.

"Since he was born. He used to have a brace for the weak leg but it only slowed him down and made him look like a robot."

Another white coat came in and they conversed quietly at the door. The new white coat sat down and watched Diwa as well. They compared notes.

Mother asked me to translate, and then insisted I tell them that Diwa was talking less only because of the medicine and the electric shocks they gave him.

"ECT? No, your son doesn't get that," the white coat said, looking at Mother.

"Yes, ECT," she repeated.

"Your son is too young for that type of therapy." He flipped through Diwa's chart.

I translated for her again, but I didn't believe them. I was sure they zapped Diwa, making him quiet just as they did in my dream. I'd dreamt that they lifted him on a gurney, bound his arms and legs with leather straps, shaved his head, and taped electrodes to it. His body convulsed while they watched his brain on a giant movie screen. With each jolt of electricity, they shorted his circuits. It was like a scene from *Frankenstein*, only in reverse.

The white coats took more of his life than they gave back. They were supposed to make him better, make him stop remembering, but they didn't. For days all he did was sit in the corner and rock or pace the perimeter of his room. On occasion he would catch and release poems. He'd been there for a week. Somehow I knew he was never coming home.

NOW

The law office is in a gentrifying part of town; half the old buildings have been torn down to make room for condominiums. From the waiting room window Diwa and I observe the construction site. Tanned men in coveralls move from machine to machine, hauling, digging, climbing steel girders, pouring concrete. Above, cranes soar and sweep their arms across the midday sky. I watch with rapt attention what it takes to build something, the men's limbs sinewy and stretched as if they too are part of the machines, flexed and accurate, precise and necessary. Mother stands next to me, her reflection overlaid on mine. She's wearing a white-and-silver embroidered salwar kameez and chunni. "It's amazing what they can do," she says. "I remember when there was nothing here but trees, and now look, this land is already on its third life." She takes off her chunni and shows me. "Do you like it?"

I nod.

"It's new. I had it made special for today. This is the first time I'm seeing you all together for so long."

I close my eyes, hoping she's not there, that she's just a construct of my unconsciousness.

"What? You don't want to speak to me now? That's okay, I can understand you even if you aren't speaking. You still don't think I'm real."

"Not today," I say under my breath so that Diwa won't hear me.

"Fine, have it your way." Then she's gone, our reflection in the window moving from three to two. We're still foreign to each other, part of an imagined past. When I mentioned this unsettled feeling to Diwa last week he said, "'We feel dreamed by someone else.'" A quote from Mark Strand. Diwa signed out the poetry book from the library and neglected to return it. He has a whole box of library books—philosophy, poetry, art, photography— that are overdue. "We should return these," I told him.

"I can't. I need them."

Those words—*I can't, I need*—have stayed with me all week. I can't do this. I need my mother. I never felt those words more intensely than I do now.

Jyoti arrives just as I sit down. She smells and looks expensive. Put together and carrying a Louis Vuitton purse. I cower into myself. I haven't washed my hair in days and I'm wearing an outfit that I bought at Costco.

"I'm not late, am I?" She checks her gold wristwatch.

"No, they haven't called us in yet."

She sits down slowly, carefully, as though she's worried about making contact with the plastic upholstered chair. "So how are you?"

"I'm fine. As fine as one can be. It's hard."

"Yeah, it is. I didn't expect it to be, but—" She shifts in her seat. "I've been meaning to call."

"But you haven't," I say, instantly regretting it when I see her face tighten. She's trying. Mother would want me to let her try.

"I should have come by," she says. "I know there's lots to figure out about the house and everything, but it's been so busy." Her phone rings and she reaches into her bag. "Hello . . . Oh, hi . . . Yes . . . No, it's fine, go ahead . . . Yeah, I think six would be good . . . Okay, I'll meet you at the school . . . Thanks for letting me know." She hangs up. "Sorry about that. I'm helping on the school parent committee this year. Trying to organize a bake sale and auction."

"A bake sale? I didn't know they still did those," I say, feigning interest.

"Oh yes, yes they do. So far we've raised three thousand dollars this year for our missionary work in Africa."

"What part of Africa?"

"Oh, I'm not really sure. But I think we may go there next year on a school trip. Even Nik may come along if he can get time away from the office, except the real estate market is so hot right now he's barely home as it is. That reminds me—he said that if we decide to sell Mother's house, he'd be happy to list it and forgo the fee, obviously."

"Very generous of him," I say stiffly. "But it's premature to be thinking about selling it just yet."

"Oh right, of course." She looks up at Diwa. "We wouldn't sell until you find a place of your own." She smiles, smacks her lips together, and pulls a strand of hair out of her lip gloss.

Diwa sits down next to me. She doesn't say anything more to him. She's like Father that way, pretending he doesn't exist, ignoring the inconvenient. When Mother was in hospice, Jyoti and I argued in sharp whispers at the foot of her bed about who would stay the night. I was tired and frayed and Jyoti hadn't been there on any of the agreed-upon days, always too busy, always finding it too hard, always leaving Diwa and me to manage on our own—until finally I confronted her. "What do you want from me?" she shot back. It felt like a slap. I didn't know how to answer. I still don't.

"Do not let God come between you," Mother says. She's sitting next to Jyoti now, flipping through a magazine. "She needs you. They both do."

The receptionist gestures to us and we file in to the windowless office. I look back for Mother but she's gone. The lawyer is an old Indian man who advertises his practice on prime-time Punjabi programming. That's where Mother got the idea to make a will. She called me one afternoon to drive her to the appointment. I didn't ask her for the details, but she told me anyway. She wanted me to be prepared.

Mr. Gupta Dusangh is sitting behind a modular wood-veneer desk with stacks of folders and Post-it notes strewn across it. He puts on his reading glasses as the receptionist hands him a file. There are only two chairs across from his desk, so I stand pressed up between the desk and the office door, leaning against what little wall space there is. While Mr. Dusangh prepares the paperwork, I make note of the various certificates and degrees that are matted and hung in ostentatious frames. They look out of place in this small, cheaply lit office. Jyoti is sitting uncomfortably straight, clasping her purse perched on her lap. We wait.

"Last Will and Testament of Amrita Kaur Sandhu—your copy," the lawyer says, handing each of us an envelope, barely making eye contact. "Very straightforward wishes; she bequeathed her possessions and her land titles in India equally among her three children with only one exception." He reads quietly in monotone legal speak: "Her principal residence is bequeathed to her only son, Diwa Singh. That's you?" he asks Diwa.

Diwa nods.

Jyoti shoots me a sideways look.

Mr. Dusangh goes on to discuss the terms of probate, and invites us back to sign a release when it completes in a few weeks. He shakes our hands without saying he's sorry for our loss, and somehow I'm relieved.

Outside in the parking lot, Jyoti pulls me aside while Diwa waits in my car.

"Did you know about this?" Her voice strains over the construction sounds.

"It's what she wanted."

"But did she ever talk about it with you? I mean, how can we know this is really what she wanted?"

"Trust me, this is what she wanted. Besides, what difference does it make to you?" I glance at her shiny new Mercedes. "It's not like you need the money."

"It's not about the money. It's the principle."

"Since when have you cared about principles?" My voice rises and I try to pull back. I try to let go, to forgive her—for not being there when Mother was sick, when Mother had fallen, when Mother needed help eating and bathing—but forgiveness feels like a failure. I'm not ready to concede.

"She did her best." Mother is standing next to Jyoti. "Everyone did. Be nice, she's your sister. Family is all you have in this life."

I ignore Mother, my eyes locked on Jyoti.

"You know I was busy. This is all really hard for me. You have Diwa to talk to. Who do I have?" Jyoti is tearing up. She fumbles in her bag, puts on her designer sunglasses, and keeps talking. I can't take her seriously, though; she looks like a bug. "Are you listening to me?"

I try to focus but can't help laughing. Finally I shake my head. "I'm sorry, I can't even—those glasses look ridiculous."

"What?" She takes them off. "Is that better? Can you listen to me now?"

I nod, pulling it together. "Remember when she couldn't stop laughing?"

"Who, Mom?"

"Oh that's right, talk about me like I'm not even here," Mother says.

"Yeah, it was the craziest thing. She just couldn't control it, or she'd laugh at all the wrong moments."

"It was awful," Jyoti says, her voice softening. "What did the doctor call it? Emotional lability?"

"Such a strange symptom. It was unsettling, to say the least."

"Unsettling? Imagine how it was for me," Mother remarks. "To have no control."

"It scared me," Jyoti continues. "The slow moving I could handle, but that—well, it's something I can't forget. It's like she stopped being her."

Mother puts her arm around her and wipes her tear-stained cheek. I watch to see if Jyoti notices, but she remains unaware.

We both fall silent, searching for something in the quiet. I imagine for a moment that we might be looking for the same thing.

"The house. Please don't make this an issue," I say. "It will only make things harder."

"It's not my intention to make things harder. I just want it to be fair." Jyoti sighs.

"It's what she wanted, it's what she thought *was* fair."

Jyoti pulls out her keys. "I have to go," she says, opening her car door. "The kids hate it when they're the last ones picked up. I'll get the bad-mom guilt trip and all that." She slides in, starts the engine, puts her sunglasses back on. Mother is sitting in the passenger seat and waves goodbye to me as they pull away. Unsettled, I return to my car where Diwa, having watched the whole scene, is waiting.

"Everything okay?" Diwa asks as I get in. "If she's mad about the house, she can have it. I never wanted it to be like this."

"No, it's fine. Besides, it's about time you had a home."

"He's been gone three weeks already. When is he coming home?" I ask. "It's so boring without him."

Mother is standing on the porch, reeling in the laundry line. "Your brother is not well," she says as she unpegs the washing. "He needs their help." She holds the sheets to her face and inhales before tossing them in the basket.

"Because of his remembering?" I heard the white coats call them voices, delusions, auditory hallucinations. They have all kinds of names for Diwa's remembering. "You know there's nothing wrong with him. He's just special. You told me so."

"It's more than that."

"What's the big deal anyway?" I'm determined to prove my point. "So what if he thinks he has a different name? Maybe he's just making things up. He's probably just saying it to get your attention. If you stop making it a big deal, I bet he'd stop. It's like when I was in kindergarten and the new girl came to school with an imaginary friend named Charlotte. She was always saying Charlotte this, Charlotte that, and acting crazy. But when the teacher finally stopped taking notice, she stopped acting weird."

"Simran, it's not the same thing."

"It might be. You don't know for sure."

"They know what to do at The Care." She's balancing the loaded basket on her hip as she walks back inside the house.

"It's not even called that. It's just a hospital for crazy people."

"It is not. Don't say such things." She dumps the load of whites on the table. "Make yourself useful and fold these." She sits down and closes her eyes for a moment. Ever since she came home from the hospital she's been tired all the time. I've been doing double the chores.

"Do I have to?"

"Simran." She makes my name a complete sentence, an entire warning.

I reach for the towels, the easiest things to fold. "If it's not a hospital, what is it then?"

"It's a place where he can stay and be safe." When Mother first told me that Diwa was going away for a few days, she made it sound nice—like an aquarium or an amusement park. But The Care is just a series of rooms in a tall grey building surrounded by green rolling fields. "Besides, he's there only until arrangements can be made."

"What arrangements?"

She continues on as if she hasn't heard me. "With the new baby, it's probably for the best." She says this as if she's convincing herself.

"He won't hurt her, if that's what you're worried about." I place my perfectly folded pile back into the empty basket. "And if you let him come home, I promise I'll take care of him. I'll make sure he's good and doesn't yell. And that he goes to school, does his homework. And I'll especially make sure that he remembers his name is Diwa and not Pyara."

"Oh, Simran, it's not like that." She hugs me. Her shoulders are shaking. When she pulls away she reaches for her handkerchief to dry her eyes. "I'm sorry. He can't come home. But we'll visit him. I promise."

"When?"

"After he gets settled in his new home. He's going to be living with your father's aunt, Bibi Jeet. You remember her?"

"Grandma's sister? She's too old to take care of Diwa. Besides, why can't he live here, with us?"

"She's not too old and we've been through this." She takes the basket to the linen closet, where she restacks my folding.

"But Diwa will be bored there. There's no one to play with and all she does is pray."

"He won't be bored. There's lots to do on the farm, and Bibi Jeet needs the help."

"What about school?"

"He'll still have school, but at home."

"School at home? That doesn't make any sense."

"It's called home school. He'll have a special tutor."

"That's the dumbest thing I ever heard." I keep arguing with her until her patience finally wears thin. It's like watching ice crack.

"Simran, enough. I said it's for the best." Her voice trembles and splits. In the other room the baby wails. "Now see what you've done. You woke your sister up. Poor thing, she's barely slept today."

I follow her into the bedroom. "You can take care of the baby and I'll take care of Diwa."

"That's *enough*, Simran," she says again, picking up Jyoti, whose face is red from crying. "It's been decided."

I watch Mother soothe Jyoti until she falls back asleep. I keep sitting there, wishing Diwa would have kept his mouth shut and never called himself Pyara and our father Manohor. After Mother leaves the room I lean over the cradle and look at Jyoti, swaddled in pink. "It's all your fault," I say and pinch her leg to make her howl.

In the months that follow, a new quiet comes over the house. It's unsettling, like the silence that wakes me up at three a.m. with the funny feeling that someone has called my name. It's as if I'm an animal sensing that something isn't right—I'm full of nervous energy, all wobbly-legged and fidgety. Mrs. Carlisle sends a note home saying that I'm not focusing and becoming disruptive in class.

Mother, preoccupied with the baby, barely glances at me when I read it out to her. She speaks sideways while cooing down at Jyoti swaddled in her arms. "Pay more attention in class, Simran, and I won't tell Father about this, okay?" She waits for me to agree.

"I wasn't doing anything wrong. The teacher just doesn't like me because I'm Indian." I'm trying out a lie.

"Don't be silly, Simran. Mrs. Carlisle is a nice teacher."

"Not anymore. She doesn't call on me when I raise my hand, and she singles me out, never punishing the other kids." I'm really stretching the truth now. "Like today. Peter put clear glue all over my desk and when my papers got stuck to it, I was the one who got in trouble."

"Did you explain it to her?"

"Yes, I said, 'But, Mrs. Carlisle, why would I put glue on my own desk? That doesn't make sense.'"

"And what did she say?"

"She gave me a detention for back-talking and wrote you this note. I think you should phone her or go talk to her." Mother hasn't been to any of the school events since Diwa went away.

"Don't be silly," she says again. "It's not necessary. Just behave in class and everything will be fine."

"But everything's *not* fine. Besides, you said we were going to visit Diwa and we haven't gone yet."

"Is that what this is about? You know Father has been working double shifts. He's tired and doesn't want to drive another two hours. It's hard enough on him driving that taxi all day."

"We could take the bus."

"Simran, it's too far away. Buses don't go that far out of the city. But don't worry, I'll talk to your father and we'll go for a visit soon."

My persistence pays off: a few weeks later we pile into Father's taxicab and drive to Bibi Jeet's farm. Father, though off-duty, still has his CB radio on and listens to the call-ins. "So many fares I'm missing," he says to Mother, who sits next to him with the baby.

"One day off is not going to make us poor." She looks out the window as we turn onto the dusty farm road.

"How much longer?" I ask. "We've been driving forever."

"Only a little while."

I wait patiently, bobbing up and down as we make our way along the gravel road. I open my backpack, triple checking that I've got everything I need: two squirt guns, a skipping rope, paper, scissors, and the book of haikus I stole from the library.

"There it is," Father says, pointing to a two-storey house that looks as though it's covered in black construction paper. There's no front yard, just dirt and a short brick fence that separates their dirt from the dusty road.

"Why's it so ugly?"

"Shh," Father says. "It just looks like this because it's not finished."

When I make a face he explains that Bibi Jeet's son is a builder, but he can work on the house only when he's not busy. "It's almost done on the inside," he assures me.

I jump out of the car and climb the fence, walking along the top as if it's a circus tightrope. "Step right up to see something amazing!"

"Simran, stop that," Mother says.

Together we walk to the front door where Bibi Jeet is waiting, a handkerchief over her mouth. Mother has told me she has asthma; I can hear it in her gaspy hello. She ushers us inside and invites us to take off our shoes. I look at the cement floor covered in a Persian rug. Father's wrong; the inside of the house is only a little better than the outside. Electrical wires jut through partly framed walls and a damp cold seeps through the visible foundation walls. "It's like jail," I whisper.

Mother shushes me then apologizes on my behalf. "She's just a child," she says. Bibi Jeet nods and we follow her up the stairs to the finished living room, complete with pink carpeting, pink drapes, and a wall covered in Guru pictures. I count the Gurus, listing them by name.

"Do you read the Gurbani?" Bibi Jeet asks. She's dressed in white, mourning since her husband's death years ago. He was on his way home from the temple when a gang of skinheads beat him to death.

"No, but Guru Nanak is my favourite," I say, chomping on my gum. "I like his grey eyes and white beard. Diwa likes Guru Har Krishan best because he was only five years old when he was named Guru. Where's Diwa? When can we see him?"

"He will be here soon," Bibi Jeet says. "He's just in the prayer room finishing his paat."

"He never used to pray."

Mother shoots me a look. "Diwa studies the Guru Granth Sahib now, Simran."

"Tea?" Bibi Jeet offers.

Mother follows her into the kitchen. Father and I wait, sitting on the velveteen settee, Jyoti cocooned in her blanket between us.

We're served tea and the Parle Gluco biscuits that Bibi Jeet brought from India. They taste stale but I eat them anyway. As the grownups talk about India, exchanging news and niceties about relatives, I lean back into the couch and peek into the next room. Diwa is sitting with his eyes closed and hands folded together, his bowed head covered with a white kerchief and his lips moving as if he's in a trance. After a moment he opens his eyes, stands up, and takes off his headscarf. Like some sort of pet, he stands at the doorway until Bibi Jeet tells him to come in.

"You need a haircut," I say, jumping up to greet him.

He runs his fingers through his chin-length hair and smiles, looking at the floor then back at me a few times.

"He's leaving his hair natural, as any Sikh should," Bibi Jeet says.

"What? So he's going to have a topknot?"

"Simran," Father warns.

"That is all right. She's just a child. It's not a topknot, child, it's a patka, and Guru Gobind Ji commands it. Isn't that right, Diwa?"

He nods and then folds his hands in greeting. "Sat Sri Akal."

I roll my eyes and sigh.

Mother calls him to her. "Come, let me see how you've grown." She places her hands on his shoulders and inspects him for a moment before embracing him. He keeps straight, partly leaning in, partly resisting.

"Can we go and play now?" I hold up my backpack.

Mother waits for Bibi Jeet to answer. "Of course, child."

Outside, Diwa shows me the farm and walks me through the blueberry bushes. "These ones aren't ready," he says, pulling back the branches, pointing to the small ones. "They don't have their crowns yet." He reaches into another bush. "But these are almost ready. See the top by the stem? It looks like a crown, right?"

"Or a topknot," I say, nudging him.

He doesn't laugh and keeps walking along the row. "Bibi Jeet says Kesh is one of the five K's and shows my devotion to the Guru. Maybe one day I'll be an Amritdhari and carry a kirpan." He slices through the bushes with his hand as if it's the sword. "Try these ones." He offers me a handful of berries.

I pop them all in my mouth at once.

"Good, right?"

I smile wide, knowing my teeth are purple. "I'm the purple people eater," I intone and chase him all the way to the barn at the back of the field. Then I bend over, my hands on my knees, catching my breath. "Wait, what's in here?"

Diwa circles back toward me.

"Nothing. Used to be where animals were but now the pickers use it for sorting."

I step inside and Diwa follows. Sun streams through broken slats, lighting the barn in uneven rays and holes. Diwa jumps from sunny spot to sunny spot as if he's playing hopscotch. Five women are in the back corner; they're busy packing produce boxes and barely look up. Flies land on their faces and they don't even notice. Diwa waves hello to the women, who smile back at him.

"You know them?"

"Yeah, sometimes I help them with the sorting. Usually on the weekends."

I cover my nose with my shirt. "It stinks in here." I walk out of the barn and make my way back through the rows of blueberry bushes.

Diwa trails behind me. "It's not that bad. You get used to it."

"Do you like it here?"

"It's okay I guess. I get to use the scale to weigh the berries and help Bibi figure out how much to pay the workers. When I'm a teenager, she says I can learn how to drive the tractor and help Uncle clear the fields. That'll be neat."

"A teenager? You won't still be here then. You should ask if you can come home with us."

"Bibi Jeet says it's not time yet. She says I have more praying to do."

"Praying for what?"

"I'm not sure."

"What do you mean, you're not sure?"

He shrugs. "I just sit there and close my eyes. The music is nice and I like the sound of the tabla. Bibi Jeet makes me parshad after."

"I hate parshad. It looks like a pile of grease and tastes like melted butter and sugar. It's gross."

"It is not," he says, shoving me into the bush.

I stumble, branches grazing my arm. "Cut it out or I won't give you your present."

"A present? What is it?"

I kneel down and pull the book from my backpack. "Haikus. I took it from the library when no one was looking. I hid it in the stack of other books I checked out. Plus, I brought you strips of paper. I even cut them just how you like them."

He keeps walking. "I don't catch poems anymore."

"Why not?" I drop the book in my pack and run to catch up.

"Bibi Jeet says I should spend my time in prayer."

"Well, maybe Bibi Jeet should mind her own business. Maybe God wants you to write poems."

"I don't think God works that way."

"So how's it work then?"

"I have to do seva. If I serve others, God will make me better."

"But there's nothing wrong with you." I grab his arm and look him in the eye. "Who are you?"

"I'm Diwa."

I smile. "Good. Now, are you still remembering?"

Diwa hesitates and picks at branches, plucking leaves as we walk by. "Sometimes. I remember things like the way you'd remember a dream, fuzzy-like."

I stop, reach into my backpack, and pull out a picture of Father's twin brother, Pyara.

"Where did you get that?"

"I found it in Mother's nightstand drawer."

"You stole it," Diwa says, his eyes wide. "That's a sin."

"Never mind that. Now tell me, is that you in the picture?"

He stares at the old photograph, shakes his head, and walks on. "I'm Diwa now."

"Now? What about before? Do you remember?" He stops again. "You do, don't you?"

He turns around and looks at me and then at the ground, his shoulders dropping.

I put my arm around his shoulder and we head back to the house. "Forget before," I say. "Pray really hard or you'll be stuck here forever."

Later that night I hear Mother and Father arguing about Diwa. I sneak out of my room to listen.

"It's been almost six months," Mother says. "Bibi Jeet says the prayers have worked. He's not remembering as much anymore."

"So?"

"So we can bring him home now."

"No, he's fine where he is."

"But what's the harm? It's time for him to come back. He's our son."

"He's doing well with Bibi Jeet. You saw it," Father says. "She needs the company, and our monthly payment helps her. What would she do without it, without him? She needs him."

I peek through the open door and notice the way they don't look at each other when they talk. Father is in bed, reading a book, the tuft of hair at the top of his head pointing up like one of my troll dolls. I can tell Mother's mad. She's at the foot of the bed, standing taller than usual, like an animal poised for a fight.

"I'm not worried about Bibi Jeet. We paid her to take care of him and she did, and now he can come home."

"Amrita." I've never heard Father use Mother's name. He never addresses her by anything but "wife." "You know I can't do it. I can't have him here. I just can't."

"But he's your son," Mother says again.

"And my brother." He looks up at her. "He's my brother and he's your—" They're quiet for a moment, staring at each other as if reading each other's mind. "What is he to you?"

She lowers her eyes as if she's embarrassed but I'm not sure why.

"What are we all to each other?" Father continues. "I don't know why God did this to us. Why he returned him to us. A punishment for what happened, maybe."

"If it is God's will," Mother says.

"I can't. It's too much for one lifetime."

I expect Mother to argue but instead she pulls back the covers and gets into bed beside him. They sit there, eyes closed, saying nothing. I realize that they're praying.

"Amrita!" Dadi ji yells. "Come inside."

"In a minute," Amrita calls from the courtyard.

"No, not in a minute." Dadi ji stomps her cane on the floor.

Amrita peers over the gate and sees Pyara coming. She rushes to the swing, picks up a book, and pretends to read as he walks in. When he smiles she nods at him from the top of the slim volume. These few moments each day sustain her.

"Rumi?" he asks.

"Pardon?"

He points to the book.

"Yes, you know it?"

"Amrita!" Dadi ji yells again.

She raises her index finger, asking him to wait, and then gets up and opens the door. "I'm coming, Dadi ji," she hollers. When she turns back, there he is holding her book, flipping through the pages, settling on a verse, his voice a bare whisper.

This being human is a guest house.
Every morning a new arrival.

He snaps the book shut and hands it to her, his fingers grazing hers. On his way inside he passes Dadi ji, who shoots him a sideways glance as she walks through the doorway. She watches him until he's out of sight.

"Amrita, I was calling you," she says. "What were you doing? Were you talking to that boy?"

"I was just reading, Dadi ji." She holds up the book. From inside the pages a note falls out and Amrita quickly retrieves it. "My page marker," she says. "Now what did you need?"

Dadi ji scowls. "I don't remember anymore." She goes back inside to her chair in front of the fan, Amrita following. "Oh, yes. I remember now. Your sari for the party is pressed and on your bed."

Once in her room, Amrita opens the slip of paper that Pyara had tucked into her book and reads:

Meet me tonight. Beyond the fields.

She reads it again, and her heart floats.

That evening, Amrita dresses with care. Her sari, an orange silk chiffon that Father bought in Bombay, drapes effortlessly. She takes a moment at the mirror, lining kohl cat eyes and squeezing her cheeks for colour. She doesn't tie her hair up in a bun the way the other girls do and instead leaves it loose, cascading down her back. She takes one more look at herself before joining her family downstairs.

"Va va!" Father claps his hands as she descends the staircase. "Beautiful."

Amrita smiles as Dadi ji turns her around, inspecting and adjusting the fall of her sari. "Very good," she says. "But your hair. This is not good." She grabs hold of it from behind and begins to braid it.

"Dadi ji, only schoolgirls wear their hair like that," Amrita says.

"And only film actresses wear their hair down. Modesty, Amrita. Modesty. What will people say when they see your hair open like this?"

Amrita yanks her hair forward and combs the braid out with her fingers. "They will think it looks nice," she says. "Father thinks it looks nice, don't you, Father?"

He shrugs. "Don't bring me into this."

"Please?"

"Oh, what difference does it make," Father says as he leads the way outside. "Let her wear her hair how she pleases. It's not as if this is *her* wedding engagement."

Dadi ji puts on her shawl and follows him out, arguing about Amrita's ability to make a good impression, make a good match, and marry a good man the entire way to the party. Amrita trails behind, thinking of nothing but Pyara.

When they arrive she tries to hide her excitement, but it lights up her eyes. As Dadi ji reintroduces her to hordes of people she hasn't seen properly for years, she scans the room for Pyara. He's standing next to his brother against the back wall. She finds herself staring at him, bridging the distance.

"Amrita!" Her friend Harjot embraces her, catching her off guard. "Isn't it exciting?"

"Isn't what exciting?" Amrita loses sight of Pyara as Harjot pulls her away.

"The engagement, of course." Harjot gestures to the elaborate decorations and show of money. "When I get married I want it to be just like this, don't you?"

Amrita looks around her at the lanterns and garlands strung through the courtyard and into the house. "Yes, it's beautiful."

"And what do you think of my new salwar kameez?" Harjot asks, twirling.

"It's as lovely as you." Amrita catches her arm mid-twirl.

Harjot laughs, and as they walk arm in arm through the packed room she fills Amrita in on the village gossip—the who-married-who and the who-did-what of daily life. Amrita nods along, but the details of dowries and weddings and babies have never interested her. "And then there's the rumour about you," Harjot says, her mouth turned up in mischief.

"What rumour is this?"

"That you will be the next to get married. And that your grandmother is already arranging your prospects."

Amrita laughs and glances over at Dadi ji, who's standing with a group of like-minded grandmothers. "There they all are, plotting and planning our lives for us."

"Poor Amrita. Did you think you could avoid it and stay in school forever? Tell me, if you had to marry one person in this room, who would it be?"

Amrita searches the room again for Pyara, but before she can answer a drum sounds. "What's that?"

"They're here!" Harjot grabs Amrita's arm and together they rush through the courtyard to witness the arrival of the caravan. The bride's family appears in their finery, carrying diwas and lanterns, trays of food and silks—an offering, a betrothal.

In the crowd behind her, someone squeezes her hand. She turns. Pyara walks on without looking back. He strides through the side gate and then up the narrow stairs toward the rooftop veranda. A few minutes later, when no one is looking, she follows. Once she reaches the veranda she can see across the fields to the banyan tree where he's waiting. She looks behind her and then descends the back stairs and makes her way toward him, her hands grazing tall grasses, her gold bangles chiming.

They stand before each other, keeping a marked distance between them. "I wasn't sure you'd come," he says.

"What if someone sees?" She looks back toward the house.

"If they haven't seen by now, they must be blind." He takes a step forward and reaches for her hand.

Her heart is racing. She pulls her hand away. "We shouldn't be doing this."

"Do you want me to go?"

She shakes her head no and yes and then no again.

"You like poems," he says, sitting on a banyan limb.

She nods. "Poems are like this tree. The words are branches that take root. The meaning can't be separated from the words, just as this tree's roots can't be separated from its branches."

"That is poetic," he says. "I wanted to study poetry, philosophy, architecture." He stands up, leaning against the trunk.

"Why didn't you then?"

"My father forbade it. Said there was little use for it. But engineering—*That is a useful profession.*" Pyara wags his finger, mocking his father's tone. "So that's what I did."

"Do you regret it?"

"I don't know. It's too soon to know. I'm too young for regrets," he says, smiling. "What did you study in college?"

"History, philosophy, poetry—not very practical for a woman."

"Studying beauty and meaning isn't practical, it's essential. How else can one make their way in the world?"

She smiles, suddenly aware of their aloneness, how nervous and excited she feels, how that combination translates in her body as fear. "And soon you'll make your way abroad. Are you looking forward to it?"

"I should say yes, but I can't say that I am."

Amrita sits on the ground and stares up at the sky. "It could be an adventure—seeing the world."

He sits down next to her. "The world is wherever you find yourself," he says as if reciting. "And here, it is. Now."

"Who wrote that?"

"Me."

"You write poems?"

"Sometimes." He catches her fleeting glance, then leans in and brushes his lips against hers. The moment is brief, but inside that moment is an entire world governed by the sound of her own pulse, of his collapsing breath on her neck.

She pulls away slowly. "I should go."

"And if you should go, where will I be but lost in this place that once was my home?"

"Did you write that?"

"Just now." He reaches for her hand. "Say you'll meet me again tomorrow."

———

The following day she waits for him to pass her on his way into the house. On that day, and each one after that, he slips a line of poetry, an invitation, into her book.

They meet each night when the moon is high and the household sleeps. She steals away unseen, unheard, and returns before dawn. They talk about things the old villagers would never speak of—politics, music, art, the future. When she's with him she feels a possibility other than her fate as someone's wife. One morning, so moved by her last encounter with him, she asks Dadi ji what she wanted to be when she was a girl. Her dadi ji looks at her with confusion. "What do you mean, child? I am what I am, and always will be. What nonsense ideas you have!"

That night, when she tells Pyara what her grandmother said, he laughs. "The world is changing, Amrita. They just don't know it yet. Anything is possible." They walk through the field together and lie down beneath the dome of sky, their bodies side by side, close but not touching. Hours pass easily.

"If you could wish for anything, what would it be?" she asks.

"Easy," he says. "I would wish to stay here with you forever."

"Not possible."

"It's true." He leans into her. "It's not possible for me to stay, but you could come with me."

"Not possible," she says again, pushing him away. "Father would never allow it."

"And why not? Our families have been friends for generations."

She sits up. "Don't make me say it."

"I'll say it for you, then. I'm not good enough. My family lacks the money and position."

"That's not true."

"You know it is. You just don't want to admit it. Your father thinks he's better than everyone and that no one is good enough for his daughter. The only thing I don't understand is why he bothered to educate you only to sell you off."

"What are you talking about? He's not selling me off. I'm not cattle."

"True, he's not selling you, he's buying you a husband. He's probably already arranging your marriage to the richest man he can find."

"He only wants the best for me."

"If that were true, he'd want you to leave this place—to go and make something of yourself."

"I am something. I don't need to be made into something." She stands. "I don't know why you're talking like this and being so cruel."

"I'm not being cruel. I'm just telling the truth. I'm the only one who tells you the truth."

"Not so. You lied to me the first day we met. When we talked about Partition, and I mentioned my mother. You said you didn't remember."

"I didn't lie. I was just a boy—I don't remember anything except for the chaos, and even if I did remember more, I would choose to forget."

"But you knew the stories about what happened to her."

"I did."

"And you stayed silent about them."

"I did and I will. Some things are best left forgotten."

"And some people are best left forgotten." She turns to leave.

"Stop," he says, taking her hand. "Why are we arguing?"

She pulls away. "I should go. The sun is coming up. Someone will see."

He gets up and takes her hand again. "I'm sorry. Let me walk with you."

They set off quietly in the pre-dawn, beneath the glow of fading stars and pale moonlight, the heavens shifting all around them.

NOW

I've decided that, this morning after breakfast, I will leave Raj. In truth, the leaving started long ago, with the drift that came with having a young child. Then came the disappointments of middle age, and now, finally, the crushing realities of mortality. Nothing is forever. I'll go after he's left for work. Meanwhile I chart our movements, track how we orbit each other, one last time. I watch him lumber out of bed, his one-armed stretch, his shuffle to the bathroom. I listen as the shower turns on, and when he's finished I stand by the mirror, letting the steam settle, as he talks about the day ahead. He goes on about this meeting and that one, deadlines and office politics, without noticing that I'm not really listening. I watch him towel off. His body is scavenger thin, all ribs and bone, meagre and vulnerable. Part of me wants to press him to my naked flesh and feel that there's still a weight to him, to the two of us, but that desire is lost just as it's realized. Instead, I brush my teeth and stare into the foggy mirror, his reflection only a hazy apparition. I make toast and he makes coffee. The television is on. "Can you believe that?" he says. Small comments on the morning's sound bites. We watch the images flash, breaking news scrolling like tickertape; it's hard to keep up. Malaysian Airlines Flight 370 disappeared shortly after takeoff last week and still hasn't been found.

"Two hundred and thirty-nine passengers on board," Raj repeats while buttering his toast. "It's crazy. How does a plane disappear?"

The news anchor, a young woman in a low-cut blouse, goes on reciting theories and outlining international search efforts, but as with all news stories these days, it leaves me empty. Raj mutes the TV and the images of distraught families, their tearful pleas, fall silent. I focus in on their faces and watch their mouths move. Soon they too will fade and disappear, rendered invisible by everyone who finds it too painful to go on looking at such tragic circumstances. "How awful," I say, wondering how it might feel to be erased, to disappear the way those two hundred and thirty-nine people did. They boarded a plane and then they were gone. Forever lost. I switch off the television as Raj gets up from the table. He rinses his coffee mug and leaves it in the sink as he has done every day of our lives.

"So what do you have planned today?" he asks as he dries his hands.

"Just the usual."

"Do you have an appointment with the therapist?"

"No. I cancelled it."

"Oh. Why's that?"

"It's been more than four months. I don't think it's helping."

"So what then?"

"I don't know. I guess I'll just go it on my own."

He pauses, and I can see his concern even though he's trying hard to stay neutral. "Maybe you could try someone new?"

"Maybe." I smile just enough to ease his worry.

He kisses me on the cheek and grabs his briefcase from the counter. "I'll see you later."

I watch him walk out, lingering in the ritual goodbye, wondering if it's so bad. Do things have to be bad to leave?

I pack the essentials. I write a note full of clichés, requesting space, time to think, a fresh start, despite knowing there is no such thing. I place the note, folded in half, on the kitchen table. I feel awful about leaving in such a small, cowardly way. I should have told him, I should have said something, he should have noticed.

"He never noticed anything. That's what you liked about him," Mother says. She's drying the dishes, pretending she belongs.

"What are you doing here?"

"I'm always here. Always listening. You think Raj has changed, but he hasn't. You're the one who's changed."

She's right. I loved that he was unfettered by drama, that he would let me be and not question me too closely. I hid my secrets in plain sight; he was satisfied by canned answers. "Fine, yes, no" suited him. I loved that about Raj, until I didn't.

"You know that leaving isn't going to help," Mother says.

"I know."

"Then why are you going?"

"Because I don't know what else to do. Besides, isn't doing something better than doing nothing?"

"Is it?"

But now she's gone again. The dishes she was drying sit in the rack, untouched.

As I collect my toiletries, I realize that Mother was right. I wanted too much.

"Of course I'm right," Mother says and hands me my makeup bag.

I take it from her without meeting her eyes. "I wish I knew that when I was in my thirties. Those years wore me down. Sharon was so young and . . ."

"And?"

"And nothing." I wonder if she knows about the affair. Do dead people suddenly know everything, having been granted a full disclosure of the past? "Why are you still here?" I ignore her until she leaves, then continue with my packing. I'm remembering how treacherous motherhood was. The small hands and feet, the wants and needs, the tears, the fits, the noise, the wide-eyed smiles that redeemed but weren't plentiful enough to maintain that tender balance. "Can't you see it?" I once said to Raj as I looked in our bathroom mirror. The erosion of my face, the dullness in my eyes. "I'm not the same."

He was in bed, typing on his laptop. "You look great," he said. "You always look great."

He never saw the dimensions or the decay, the moth-eaten ideas I had of myself. He'd comment only on the ruins of home. "This house is a mess. What have you done all day? What about dinner?" It was a relief to go back and finish my degree once Sharon had settled into her preschool routines, but even then I felt guilt as easily as Raj felt fatigue. He'd be tired from his day and I'd be troubled about not being there for Sharon.

The affair began shortly after I started working at the hospital. It was casual and meaningless but the only thing I had that was my own. Skin on skin in the afternoon, high-thread-count sheets, expensive hotels. It was all I wanted—an antidote to domestic life, the clamouring of a child, the sleeping-on-my-own-side-of-the-bed marriage. Charles was a good man. Not married, or perverted, or playboyish, he was just like me, looking for a mooring. Neither of us ever discussed our lives beyond our work at the hospital or beyond the sex. There was nothing salacious about it. When he left for a position on the East Coast, saying goodbye was surprisingly easy. No promises were made, no plans to continue. He simply disappeared from my life. As the years went by I wondered if he was even real or if I'd made the whole thing up. I could barely remember the way he looked, or felt. Just the blue of his eyes looking into the dark of mine. Something electric and lonely. Last year I heard he'd died in a motorcycle accident. I never even knew he had a motorbike. He left behind a wife, two children, and me. He left me behind long ago. For days it seemed strange that I'd made love to a man who was now dead. An intimacy erased. No one would ever know.

Now, with my bag packed, I walk through the house, surveying years in long, panoramic looks. I leave behind a life poorly conceived and only partly built.

"I don't want to wear this," I say, tossing the salwar kameez at Mother. "It's stupid. Every time they come you expect us to put on some show."

She picks up the Indian suit and places it on the bed. "I didn't ask if you wanted to wear it. Now put it on before your father hears you arguing. You know he's tired."

"He's always tired." I'm looking in the mirror now and see Jyoti dumping my makeup bag on the floor. "Hey, cut that out!" Mother grabs the red lipstick before she can draw on herself.

Jyoti stamps her feet. "Give it back! I want to be a clown."

Mother shushes her and turns to me. "Where did you get this?"

I'm kneeling down to pick up the shimmering eye shadow pallets. "Where do you think? The store, of course."

"But where did you get the money? Did you take it from my purse?"

"Mother, it's not a big deal. It's a few bucks. All the kids wear makeup."

"No, not all the kids. Not you. You are only fourteen. Too young for this." She pockets the lipstick.

"Too young for this," Jyoti parrots in her preschool way.

"Look, please just get ready," Mother says. "We can talk about this later. They'll be here soon."

"What's the point?" I say as she's about to leave.

"The point is that he's your brother and we haven't seen him in a long time."

"And whose fault is that?"

"Simran, that's enough."

"No, really, you make such a big deal of these visits and then you send him away again. I don't get it."

"Lower your voice," she says in a harsh whisper. "I told you your father's tired. He's sleeping."

"More like sleeping it off," I mumble.

"Ten minutes, Simran. They'll be here in ten minutes." Mother picks up Jyoti and carries her out of the room. I shut my door behind them, strip down in front of the mirror, and look at myself in my beige granny panties. I haven't started wearing a bra even though I need one. Mother doesn't seem to notice that I'm getting older. She wasn't even ready for me when I told her I got my period last year. I expected some kind of embarrassing motherly talk like the other girls at school got from their moms, but I got nothing but a pad and a belt handed to me.

I sigh and put on my pink salwar kameez. It's tighter around the chest than it was last time I wore it. I drape my chunni in the front so that no one can see my buds. *Buds.* That's what the boys at school call them because they're not big enough to be boobs or tits. Rodney tried to bud-twist me in the hallway the other day, but I got him back by kneeing him in the groin.

Mother knocks. "Are you ready?"

I open the door. "Happy?" I ask, twirling.

"Very," she says. "Your brother will be pleased to see you."

"How long was he in India?"

"Six months. They toured the temples."

"Lucky them," I say, glancing at my bedroom walls covered in posters of Gurus and temples. I tried to put up a few *Tiger Beat* Duran Duran posters but Mother wouldn't have it.

"Yes, he's lucky. Just because he has a different life doesn't mean it's not a good life." She ushers me down the hallway as the doorbell rings. Father is sitting in the living room. He smells of menthol and aftershave, a combination meant to cover his liquor breath. He's been drinking the hard stuff, and it shows. His eyes are always red and he has a tremor that's apparent when he holds his glass. When Diwa and Bibi Jeet come in, Father stands up and folds his hands. "Sat Sri Akal." He doesn't hug Diwa. He shakes his hand and presses a twenty-dollar bill in his palm. Diwa tries to give it back but Father insists. Mother tells everyone to sit down, be comfortable. She asks me to get tea. While I'm in the kitchen I hear their chatter—polite and strained.

"Say hello to your brother," Mother says. I peek into the living room, where she has Jyoti sitting on Diwa's lap.

"Hello, brother," Jyoti repeats dutifully. Then she jumps off his lap and everyone watches as she unpacks her tea set and begins to play make-believe. Diwa makes slurping sounds as he sips the imaginary tea from the plastic cup. Jyoti laughs and copies him.

"So, the trip. How was it?" Mother asks.

"Very good," Bibi Jeet replies. "The weather was good. After the tours, we spent some time in our village for a week. He met all the relatives."

I bring in the tray of tea and biscuits and set it down in front of Diwa. He's gotten taller, and although he's only nine he's got some scruff on his face, the beginnings of a moustache. He looks like the ESL kids at school, all greasy-like in their topknots and Kmart clothes. He's wearing a velveteen zip-up cardigan and brown cords—definitely clearance rack.

"I'm glad he was able to see the house where he was born." Mother speaks deliberately, glancing at Father.

"Of course, he doesn't remember the place," Bibi Jeet says. "He hasn't been there since he was a baby."

"Yes, we never were able to go back after that." Mother's smile is relieved: Diwa hasn't remembered things he shouldn't.

"Manohor, your parents were happy to see us. Though they were understandably upset that they were never able to join you in Canada."

"Yes, well, their application was denied. You know we tried."

"And your father," Bibi Jeet continues, motioning to Mother. "He sends his regards."

"Of course." Except for the occasional strained long-distance phone call, Mother hasn't spoken to her father. She turns to Diwa, wanting to change the subject. "How are your studies? Have you managed to keep up?"

Bibi Jeet answers for him. "He's doing fine. Once he gets to the middle grade, I will put him in the local school. The bus comes right by our house."

"That's a good idea," Father says. "He should be around children his own age. Very important for the socialization."

"Actually, I have some books he may like," I say.

My parents stare at me as if they've forgotten I was in the room.

"Can I show them to him?"

"Of course, of course," they say in unison, their voices trailing as Diwa follows me down to the basement rec room.

"You're welcome," I say and flop onto the beanbag chair.

"Welcome for what? Where are the books?"

"There are no books, dummy. I was just rescuing you from snoresville upstairs."

"Oh. What's a snoresville?"

"Sit down, will ya. Relax." I motion to the couch. "So how are you really?"

"I'm fine."

"Fine? Just fine? I haven't seen you for six months and that's all you have to say?"

His eyes light up. "I bought you a present from India." He reaches into his pocket and hands me a small red velvet bag. Inside is a gold ring.

"Is it real?" I ask, trying it on.

"I think so. At least the man at the store said it was."

"How did you buy it?"

"Saved my chore money."

I'm impressed. "Thanks," I say, admiring it.

"I figure it'll remind you of me. So you don't forget."

"I won't forget. Hey, can I ask you a question?"

"Sure."

"Do you like all this God, religious stuff?" I gesture to his topknot.

He shrugs. "I don't know."

"Well, I think it's dumb. Father doesn't have a turban, so why should you?"

He shrugs again.

"We should cut your hair," I say, leaning forward.

"I don't think they'd like that very much." Diwa points upstairs.

"Who cares what they like. Why should everything be about them? It's time to rebel."

"Rebel?"

"Yeah, take a stand."

"Huh?"

"You know, take a stand, make a statement. Show them that just because they won't let you stay here doesn't mean they can control you." I'm pacing back and forth now as if I'm in the army.

"Bibi Jeet says it's better that I stay with her."

"Of course she'll say that. She's one of them."

"Them?"

"Yes, them, meaning not us. Come on." I lead him to the small, dingy basement bathroom and then drag a stool in. "Sit down."

"What are you going to do?"

"Just trust me. We need to update your look." I undo his patka, loosening his bun until his hair unwinds down his back.

"Holy shit, it's so long," I say, brushing his mane. His eyes are wide, surprised that I cursed. "All the kids at school swear. Believe me—when you go to middle school you'll want to blend in."

"Why?"

"Because," I say emphatically. "You just will."

"Is that why I should cut my hair?"

"Precisely." I pat him on the shoulder. "I'll be right back." I rush to the basement room where Mother keeps her sewing machine and rifle through the drawers until I find her shears. "Are you ready?" I say, returning with the scissors in hand.

He swallows hard and nods.

Gathering his hair in one hand and opening the scissors in the other, I count down from three.

Diwa clenches his eyes shut on "one."

"Simran? Are you here?" Mother calls. I drop the scissors as she opens the door.

"What are you doing? What's happening?"

"Simran is going to make me look like all the other kids. So I'll fit in at school," Diwa announces.

"Is that so?" Mother tells him to put his hair back in its top-knot. Then she picks up the scissors and pulls me out of the room. "What were you thinking?"

"Me? I'm just helping him."

"Well, this," she says, holding up the scissors, "is not *helping*. Your father and I are the ones who decide what's best for your brother."

"Right, because sending your only son away for years is such a good decision."

Mother's face is pained. "Simran, what's gotten into you? Since when do you talk like this?"

I shrug. "Since now."

"Go to your room." Her arm is outstretched, pointing the way. "And stay there for the rest of the day."

"Whatever." I turn back. "Bye, Diwa. See you next time."

I sit on the small patch of floor between the two double beds in my room, listening to my cassette player so that I don't have to hear them pretend at small talk. After some time, Mother comes in and sits on the bed across from me.

I take off my headset and stop the tape. "Are they gone?"

"Yes. I told them you weren't feeling well."

"Are you going to tell Father?" I'm barely meeting her eyes.

She shakes her head. "I think it's best if we forget about it. No need to upset him."

"Forgetting—that's what we do best." I pop my headphones back on.

Mother yanks them off just as I'm about to press play. "What's that supposed to mean?"

I push her away. "Just because Diwa has forgotten what happened doesn't mean that I have. You've practically disowned him . . . He's your *son*."

"We haven't disowned him."

"Call it whatever you want, but he's not here with us, his real family, is he?"

"Simran, don't speak of things you don't understand."

Her voice is raised and forceful, but I don't back down. "Look, I'm just saying that I can't forget as easily as the rest of you."

She kneels down in front of me, cups my cheeks in her hands, and squeezes like a vise until I'm forced to look at her. "Well then, perhaps you should try harder. Because sometimes forgetting is the only thing that gets you through this life."

"It's probably Raj," I say, looking at my phone display.

"You can't keep avoiding him." Diwa glances up from his spot on the couch where all day he's been listening to my excuses for leaving Raj. Unlike Mother, he has no remedy, no advice, just a sage's ear.

I wait until the rings stop. "I don't know what to say."

"Tell him what you told me. That you just need a break." The phone starts ringing again and I click it to silent. "He's not going to stop calling until you answer." Diwa counts down from five, and on cue the house phone rings. "If you're not going to answer it, I will."

I let him take up the cause, listening to his tentative hello, his pretend surprise that it's Raj, the "How are you" and "I'm fine" niceties.

"Simran? Yeah, she's here. Let me get her for you." Diwa covers the speaker as he hands it to me. "It'll be fine. Just tell the truth." He disappears down the hall.

I wait until he's out of earshot before answering. "Hello."

"I read the note," Raj says.

I don't know how to answer.

"Are you staying at your mother's house?"

"Yeah."

"I'm coming over."

"No, don't. There's no point." I'm staring out the window. Outside it's grey, but the trees are budding, flashes of bright green and pink—beginnings again.

"What do you mean, there's no point? You leave me this note and you think that's it? That I'm just supposed to *take* it? What about me?" There's something urgent and panicked in his voice, and in a way I'm relieved that his evenness, his endless calm, is unravelling.

"What about you?" I turn away from the window and sit in my mother's lift-assist armchair, bracing for whatever comes next.

"Exactly. You've said your piece, or at least you've written it. Now it's my turn."

"Okay, that's fair. So go ahead." I swallow hard, preparing for him to tell me that I'm selfish and immature, but he doesn't say anything. "Well?" I've been fiddling with the chair's remote control buttons, and now I recline all the way back so that I'm staring at the ceiling.

"Go ahead and what?" he says.

I'm still staring at the ceiling, remembering how my mother would fall asleep in her chair in this exact position. "Tell me how you feel."

"Spare me the sarcasm. I don't know what I ever did to make you so unhappy."

I curl into the plush chair. "I never said I was unhappy."

"No, you're right, you never did say that. You just blindsided me instead. What am I supposed to believe when I come home and you're gone?"

I pause for a long moment. "I don't know."

"You don't know. That's all you ever say anymore."

"I'm sorry, okay? I just need a break." I press the buttons on the chair at random, the chair lifting up, down, and forward.

"A break? Isn't that what this has been? It's been five months since she died. I mean, you haven't worked. And you don't do much around the house—you just sit around watching daytime TV or spend hours online researching the afterlife, ghosts, and reincarnation."

I feel heavy with shame and armour. "I didn't realize you were keeping tabs."

"What else was I supposed to do? If you wanted privacy you should have cleared your search history. And even then, knowing all that, I still don't ask anything of you. I don't push. Everyone I've talked to says you're just grieving, so I don't push—I give you your space and still you up and leave."

"Everyone? Who's everyone? So you've been going around *talking* about me?"

"It's not like that. I was concerned is all."

"You couldn't possibly understand." I'm shaking my head again.

"You're right, I don't. I don't understand because you won't talk to me. You don't tell me anything."

Silence.

"What should I tell Sharon?" he asks.

"Nothing. I'll let her know I'm staying here and just need some time. I'm sure she'll understand."

"Fine. I'll leave it with you then."

We stay on the line, breathing quietly for a moment. Mother's cuckoo clocks mark the hour, chimes ringing from room to room as if she's sounding the alarm, trying to tell me that I'm running out of time.

"So what now?" he asks.

"I'm not sure." I move the chair to an upright position.

"So I just wait. I just keep waiting . . . for how long?"

"I'm sorry," I say, getting up from the chair. "I wish I could tell you."

"Me too." Then the line goes dead.

I listen to no one being on the other end before I hang up. Part of me wants to call him back, but what is there to say but "I'm sorry"? I put the phone on the table and wander into the kitchen. Mother is at the stove making tea. She's older today, with silver hair and olive skin; she looks the way she did before she got sick.

"Now what?"

"That's no way to greet me in my own house," she says. "Do you want a cup of tea?"

"Sure." I hand her two cups.

"That was the wrong thing to do, you know."

"I know."

"He's a good man."

"That's not what you used to think." I stare at her, telling myself that she's not real, that she is real, not quite sure which truth I prefer.

"What can I say? I was wrong. He turned out all right. But you . . ."

"Always a but. I know—I'm the problem."

She strains the tea through the sieve. "He can't help you with this. Don't lay it on him."

"I'm not."

"What are you doing?" Diwa asks.

I startle and almost knock the cups off the counter. "Shit! Sorry, I didn't hear you come in." I look around the room but Mother's gone and the stove is untouched, no trace of the tea she was pouring. "I was just going to put some tea on. Do you want some?"

He nods. "Everything okay? I mean with Raj. You seem upset."

"As okay as it can be, I guess. We'll just have to see." I turn the stove on. "Do you mind me staying here?"

"No, of course not. I like the company. Besides, you can help me sort through some of Mother's things. I don't know what to do with it all."

"Yeah, I suppose it's time." I look at the panelled wall covered in her collection of souvenir spoons. "She had every province except for PEI. She always wanted to go there and see the Anne of Green Gables house."

"She loved that movie."

"It's a shame she never actually saw any of these places." I scan the provinces and states inscribed on the spoon handles. "She never went anywhere. All she did was collect stuff . . . Do you ever wonder why?"

"I think people who've lost everything collect things," Diwa says. "It's a natural response. Street people do it—and then even when they have a home, they still keep things. I knew a guy who collected boxes, just in case he had to live in one again."

"That's so sad."

"And practical."

"Did you keep things?"

"No."

"Why?"

He looks around as if taking stock. "Holding on makes it hard to move on."

BEFORE

"Is it true?" Amrita's father asks. He's staring out the window, his back to her. When she doesn't answer, he turns around. "Is it true? What they say about you and the boy, Pyara?" His voice is loud and assaulting.

"What do they say?" Amrita glances back at Dadi ji, who sits quietly on the settee in the corner of her father's study.

He slams his hand against the desk. "You will make me say it?"

"We have done nothing." This is partly true. There has been nothing physical between them since the kiss. Nothing but words and restraint. "We are friends. There is no shame in that."

"Ha, no shame," Dadi ji says, snickering. "The servants gossip, and the village is clucking like chickens satisfied by the sordid details of our failings."

Father shoots his mother a look. "And tell me, daughter, what are people to think of this friendship? This familiarity? This sneaking around like thieves in the night. Did you think no one would notice? What are they to think?"

"I don't care what people think."

"Well, you should. And what about what I think? Do you care about that? Do you care about our honour?"

"Of course I do. I never meant to hurt anyone."

"You never meant it? You were never meant to behave this way. All I gave you—an education, privilege—you threw it away."

"I didn't throw it away."

"Stop talking!" He walks over, grabs her by the ear, pulls her close. "From now on you will listen to me." Her body bends toward his, his heavy breath in her ear. "From here on, you will do as you are told. Understand?" He pushes her away and she nods fearfully, cowering in the corner until Dadi ji coaxes her away to her room.

Over the next days her father doesn't take his meals with Amrita; he barely even acknowledges her. She hears from the servants that, without explanation, Pyara has been told his services are no longer required. "What did you expect?" Dadi ji says. "Did you expect us to be happy? Do you expect forgiveness?"

"I don't know. I wasn't thinking."

"No, you weren't thinking. Your head is too full of movies and silly books. You have to face reality, Amrita."

"But what is to be?"

"Your father must do what he believes is right, and if you want his forgiveness, you must follow and do whatever he asks of you."

Later that evening Amrita throws herself at her father's feet, a dutiful act of humility and respect. He says nothing, stepping away as if she were an animal. In the next days, his only response to her continued apologies is silence. And over the course of the following month, despite her attempts to atone, she is confined to the house. She is lost to him.

"She belongs to someone else now, as is the way with all daughters." This is what she hears him tell Dadi ji the night he summons her once again to his study.

She sits in the cane chair across from his desk, waiting for him to say something. The two windows behind him are open, the sheer draperies billowing in. He leans against the desk next to her.

"I have spoken to Pyara's father, Pa ji Surag, about what has happened between you and his son."

Amrita stares at her feet. She's heard the servants gossiping about the day Father confronted Pyara's family—the shame of it all.

"Pa ji Surag is a good man. I have known him for many years. Since before you were born."

Amrita does not dare look up.

"Neither of us condones this friendship, but we accept responsibility for it. We should have been more careful. We should have known. But now that we do, we have settled it so that both families can save face. Since there is no hope of you making a better match, I have no choice." He sits down at his desk and, not looking at her, he continues: "The arrangements have been made. You will marry the boy and go abroad with him. You will leave this place. You will start a new life."

She hides her surprise and summons decency. "Yes, Father."

"Until then, you are not to see him. You are not to leave this house unescorted. Understand?"

"Understood."

As promised, she is never left alone. But Amrita's servant, Ruby, a romantic, foolhardy girl of sixteen, takes pity on her and agrees to deliver notes to Pyara. For weeks they share a written correspondence. Always simple. A few lines. Just words back and forth.

They don't know that these lines, these letters, promises delivered, would soon be all they have left of each other.

Diwa's room is just the way he left it. Toys in the bins, Hot Wheel tracks on the carpet, and colouring books on the desk. Even when he came and stayed over, nothing in the room ever changed. I open the window, letting the winter air neutralize the musty stink of shut-ins and mothballs. I'm piling the toys into an empty box when Mother comes in. She's still wearing her housecoat even though it's six o'clock in the evening. Ever since Father went on sick leave she's given up; she's taken to wandering around the house in her pyjamas all day.

"What are you doing?" she asks.

"What does it look like I'm doing? I'm cleaning up."

She grabs the box from me and sets it on the desk. "It's fine the way it is." She takes the toys out one at a time, looking at each carefully before putting it back where it was.

"He doesn't even come home anymore. It doesn't make sense to keep it like this."

"I like it this way."

"That's not fair. I'm seventeen and I shouldn't have to share a room with a six-year-old. Especially when this room is empty."

"This room is not empty."

"No, only because you keep it as a shrine."

"I keep it how I want it. This is still my home." She slides the window shut, and for a moment it feels as if all the air has been sucked out of the room.

"I know. Your house, your rules."

"Ha! Since when did you listen to my rules? You do as you please, always wandering around with boys, coming home late. You have no respect for our family."

"What family?" I say, laughing. "If you haven't noticed, one of us is missing."

"He's not missing."

"Well he's not here in his room, is he?"

Mother folds her arms across her chest and doesn't answer.

"Fine, whatever. You can keep your shrine, I don't care." I head out of the room and then down the stairs, grabbing the car keys on the way.

"Where are you going?" Mother says, running down behind me.

I yank on my running shoes. "Out!" I yell, rushing through the doorway.

I turn on the ignition. The engine rattles and chokes. Barefoot and crazed, Mother runs after me and bangs on the car window. "Open up," she yells repeatedly, pounding the glass with her fist.

I turn the key again, flooring the gas. The engine revs and I quickly reverse, driving away inside a plume of exhaust smoke. In the rearview mirror I can barely make out my mother's silhouette in the haze, but I know she must be standing there in the middle of the street watching me. I pull out my father's cigarettes, the ones he keeps hidden under the seat, and hold the wheel straight with one hand while grabbing the lighter from the glove compartment with the other. The car swerves; an oncoming car honks and weaves out of the way. I pull over, light the cigarette, and take a drag. I don't even like the taste, but something about breathing the smoke in and out calms me. I roll down the window and tap the ashes, then toss out the smouldering butt before heading to the underpass where all the kids hang out. I park my car at the top of the ravine and trek downhill to the base of the bridge. The usual party is underway—heavy metal music blaring, a small fire, people standing around exchanging tokes. I walk into the circle of smokers. "Where's Johnny?"

A girl with an off-the-shoulder neon top points behind her. The new girl at school is sitting on his lap.

"Hey," I say, walking over. "What the fuck?"

Johnny whispers something in the new girl's ear, making her laugh that kind of thrown-back-head, hair-toss howl. She kisses him hard and then slides off his lap and saunters by me.

"What about it?" he says as he reaches into his cooler. He's glassy-eyed, drunk or stoned. "Chill out, have a beer." He hands me one and part of me wants to take it, to accept it as if it were an apology. Instead I knock it out of his hand. The kids around us gasp in exaggerated unison. Johnny's chest puffs up; it looks like he's about to lose it. But he sees the others watching so he leans back in his chair and laughs me off, pretending he's too cool to care.

"I thought you and I—"

"You thought wrong." He opens his beer can and takes a swig.

I watch him, not knowing what to say. Behind me, kids are

laughing. Someone yells, "This is my favourite song!" and turns up the music.

"What do you want me to tell you?" Johnny asks as he gets up, his six-foot frame towering over me. He grabs me by the back of my neck and kisses me. "It was fun, you know. But it was a one-time thing."

I push him away. "Fuck you, *Jugdeesh*," I say, using his real name to piss him off.

"It's Johnny." He points to the lettering on his varsity jacket.

"Whatever." I walk past the kids who are high and yelling, "Jugdeesh!" over and over again as if his name were a war cry.

"It's Johnny, for fuck's sake!" I hear him shout.

I make my way back through the dark to the car. I sit with the engine on and the radio playing, wondering how I could have been such an idiot. To Johnny, I was just a quick backseat lay, something to do until someone better came along. I close my eyes for a minute. I don't want to go home. I don't want Mother to be right; I don't want the I-told-you-so, I-know-best, listen-to-me, you're-too-young-to-understand bullshit. So I drive into the night, speeding along until I get to the narrow dirt road that leads to the farm, to Diwa.

I haven't been here for years. Somehow everything seems different—smaller and darker. I creep forward, careful not to veer into the ditches that run along both sides of the road. I park out front of Bibi Jeet's dilapidated house, trying to remember if it always looked this bad or if it's just the darkness that makes it look so abandoned. Some of the clapboard siding is missing and one of the decorative shutters on the big front window is falling off, hanging lopsided on its hinge. The front light is on but the rest of the house blends into the night. As I get out of the car I realize that I'm frightened, but I'm not sure why. I exhale and pound on the front door, calling Diwa's name. "It's me, open up!" I call out again and again. Finally, he appears.

"What are you doing here?"

"Is Bibi inside?"

"No, she's at the temple." He opens the door a bit wider and I push my way in.

"Good, get your things. I'm taking you home."

"What are you talking about?" His hair is wet and tangled, hanging past his shoulders. When he sees me looking he quickly ties it up. I want to tell him to leave it, that it's nice, but I don't.

"No time for explanations." I head to his basement bedroom. "Fuck, look at this place. This is where you sleep?" A single mattress lies on the floor, a dresser is stacked with books, and an old black-and-white TV is playing an *I Love Lucy* rerun. Despite the antennae, the screen is half snow and squiggly lines. When I turn it off the image collapses into a single dot. Silence now except for the fuzzy sound of static. "Remember when we were kids and we'd stick our faces against the screen to feel the electricity?"

"No."

I smile. "You were probably too small to remember. Come on, let's get you out of this dump."

"It's not so bad. Most kids would love to have a TV in their room."

I pull on the dresser drawer, jiggling it until it opens. "Grab your bag," I tell him as I empty the drawer, throwing its contents in a pile on the mattress.

He doesn't move.

"Come on, let's go."

"Go where?"

"Home." I can feel my eyes widening, imploring him. "It's time to come home."

"This *is* my home now." He sits down on the mattress.

"No, it's not. They might want you to think that, but it's not. Besides, I *want* you to come home." I open the closet door and grab his duffle bag.

He shakes his head. "I like it here."

"No you don't. How could you? Look at this place—it's a shit-hole in the middle of nowhere."

"I'm used to it. I know what to expect. Besides, Bibi needs my help."

"She'll be fine without you." I start to pile his clothes into the bag.

He grabs the bag. "No. Doctors say she's sick. I can't leave her. She'd be alone."

"Are you kidding? You believe that shit?"

"She's been like a mother to me," he says. "I can't leave."

"No, she's brainwashed you is what she's done. The doctors told them you were sick and that's why you're here. Don't you remember? But they were wrong. There was never anything wrong with you."

"I can't leave," he says again and stands up. It's the first time I realize that he's taller than me. His eyes are sad but resolute.

"Fine, you want to stay, then stay." I drop his bag on the floor. "But don't come crying to me when you want to come back," I add, yanking off the gold ring he gave me and throwing it at him. He scrambles to grab it as I rush down the hallway.

"Wait, Simran, where are you going?"

"Home."

It's the last thing I say to him.

PART
TWO

THEN

Jyoti breezes into the kitchen clutching a Bible in one hand and sneaking two shortbread cookies with the other.

"Not before dinner, it will spoil your appetite," Mother says.

Jyoti places her Bible on the table and lays one of the round cookies on her tongue. She closes her eyes.

"What's she doing?" I ask.

"Sacrament." Mother rolls her eyes.

"Jesus Christ—for real?"

Jyoti opens her eyes and closes her mouth, biting down. Mouth full, she says, "Don't take the Lord's name in vain."

"For goodness sake, Jyoti," Mother says. "We're not even Christian, or Catholic, or whatever you're playing at now."

"You're doing it again. Goodness is close to Godness and that's close to God, so that's twice in vain." She closes her eyes once more and prays. "Dear Father, forgive my mother and my sister, Simran." She sticks her tongue out at me. "They know not what they say."

"That's right, Jyoti, pray for us," I say, laughing.

"It's not a joke!" Jyoti storms out, reciting chapter and verse.

"What was *that* all about?"

Mother sighs, then gets up to pour herself a glass of water. "Last week she came home and said she was baptized in Christie's swimming pool."

"Christie? The kid who used to eat glue?"

"That's the one. Jyoti took my fake pearls, the ones your father bought me, and asked if she could use them as a rosary. I said yes. I thought they were just playing a game. You know, like the way you played dress-up? But then Mrs. Shum told me she'd been confessing her sins at the local Catholic churches and riding around on her bike handing out crucifixes she made out of twigs."

"Are you serious?"

Mother nods and takes a few gulps of water.

"What are you going to do about it?"

"Nothing. I'm hoping she'll grow out of it. She's only nine. You know, it's a . . . How do you say it in English?"

"A phase."

She snaps her fingers. "Yes, that's it, a phase."

"That's very reasonable of you. I don't remember you being so forgiving of my phases."

She sits back down at the kitchen table. "How could I be? You had so many."

"It wasn't that bad."

"First it was punk and blue hair, then it was short skirts, staying out late, boys," she says, counting them on her fingers. "So many boys."

"That's all normal teen rebellion."

"Not where we're from; in India you listen to your parents."

"Well, we're not in India anymore."

"No, you're right about that. But living in this country—well, it's had its own hardship."

I know we're talking about more than we say. Diwa's been gone for over a year. He ran away after Bibi Jeet died. He was only fourteen. We haven't seen him since.

Mother's eyes are full, brimming with memory. She wipes them with the back of her hand and smiles. Jyoti is still reciting scripture in the other room. "Keep it down!" Mother yells. "God can hear you even if you don't speak."

I laugh.

"Oh well, at least with Jyoti, I know where she is. But with you—so much worry. It's a wonder you've found a man to marry you." She motions to Raj, who's in the other room attempting to talk to Father even though Father has no idea who he is. He barely remembers any of us anymore.

Mother gets up again and opens the kitchen cupboard, pulling out the dinnerware. I set the table, lining up forks and knives.

"I wish you would have told us about Raj sooner. If I'd known about him, I wouldn't have made inquiries for you."

"Inquiries?"

"At the temple. I asked the ladies there to let me know of any eligible boys for you."

"Did you find any?" Raj asks from the doorway. He flashes me a smile, a thunderbolt to my heart. Always on target.

"Dozens." Mother laughs. "But there is no need for that. Times are changing, and now girls and boys find each other themselves."

"Did you have an arranged marriage?" Raj asks.

Mother is at the stove pouring daal into a serving dish, her back to us now. "Of course I did. That's how it was in those days. You did what your parents asked you to do." Her voice is wilting. "You believed that they knew what was best."

Silence, except for Jyoti's prayers.

"Raj's parents met at college in Delhi," I offer.

"New Delhi," Mother repeats.

"They were studying medicine," Raj puts in.

"Both doctors." Mother is impressed. "And how do they feel now that you're marrying my doctor daughter?"

"Hardly—I haven't even finished my undergrad yet," I say.

"They're happy about it. Really supportive. They've even offered to help with the baby so Simran can keep going to school."

Mother stops what she's doing and stares at us.

"That is, when we have kids," Raj says quickly, realizing that I haven't yet told her about the baby.

"Bit early to be thinking about children, isn't it?" She hands me the serving dishes. "First priority is getting into med school. And then, when she's settled in her career, then is the time for babies."

"Of course," Raj says.

I lay out the dishes and call Jyoti to dinner. Mother speaks to Father gently, telling him it's time to eat. He's agitated, confused, his voice trailing to nothing, his eyes large and pleading. The dementia has aged him. His face and body have grown frail—he's just skin hanging from bone. In some ways it seems that even his body has forgotten him. He looks around the room, and when he sees us in the kitchen looking back his eyes well and spill. He cries softly, muttering to himself. Mother tells him he doesn't have to eat if he doesn't want to and brings him his dinner on a tray table.

Jyoti rolls her eyes. "Here we go again."

"Jyoti," I say, imploring her to stop.

Mother sits down at the table. I wait for her to make mention of Father's dementia. "So, have you thought of a wedding date?" she says instead.

"Wait, we have to say grace." Jyoti bows her head, whispering, "Thank you, Father, for the food."

"That's enough, Jyoti," Mother warns, and we continue to pass the dishes.

"We haven't set anything yet," Raj says, looking at me. "We wanted to discuss it with you."

"And what about your family? Do they want you to have a traditional Sikh wedding?" Mother asks.

"They don't really mind. As long as we're happy."

"That's very modern of them."

"They just want me to be happy this time."

Mother looks confused. "This time?"

Raj stammers and I interrupt. "Raj was married once before. Didn't I tell you?"

"No, you forgot that detail." Mother raises her eyebrows, forcing a strained smile.

"It was an arranged marriage. It didn't last," Raj says.

"Clearly." Mother chews deliberately. "Do you mind if I ask what happened?"

"Mother," I say.

"What? I have a right to know." She turns to Raj. "After all, you are marrying my daughter."

I try to stop this line of questioning. "What smells so good?"

"Saag paneer." She keeps her eyes on Raj. "Your favourite."

The room is silent and heavy.

Raj puts down his fork. "I love your daughter very much . . . and as for my first marriage, well, it was just something that happened to me. It wasn't what I wanted. My parents arranged it and I went along. My older brother had left and done what he wanted, so . . ."

"So you did the right thing? Played the part of the dutiful son?"

"Yes. It turned out to be a mistake."

"How old are you?"

"Mother . . ."

"What, I can't ask his age?"

"No, of course you can," Raj says. "I'm thirty."

"Thirty?" Jyoti has suddenly tuned in to the conversation. "That's so old!"

"It *is* quite an age difference. A decade." Mother pauses. "And do you have children?"

"Mother, for God's sake!"

"Stop taking the Lord's name in vain," Jyoti says.

"No, I don't have any children," Raj says. He is calm and patient; nothing Mother says seems to bother him. Even when she asks how we met, why he wants to marry me, what he could possibly have in common with me given the age gap, he remains steadfast. I like this about Raj. Nothing fazes him, not even my pregnancy. Right from the start he said he wanted to do the right thing, and proposed marriage. Even though we'd been on a break when I told him, he didn't question my fidelity—and in that moment he made me believe his version of me. I was better than my drunken one-night stand, even though that one night had been better than every night of my life. It wasn't the sex that had made it feel like that, or the conception that may have came from it—it was the simplicity of it. The Wanting. The Having. The Letting Go. I think of that man almost every time I sleep with Raj; I try to make it feel as urgent and desperate as it felt that night. But it's rarely like that with him, and when he falls asleep I lie there in the dark, hands between my legs, hostile and guilty.

I never tell him that the baby might not be his.

Within a month we're married, and everything that was, all those other parts of my life, drift away. I become an island.

At thirty-two weeks, I lose the baby.

It's stillborn, dead and yet tethered to me. I realize then that in life there is no letting go.

As I sit next to Diwa drinking my morning coffee, I delete the most recent message from the funeral home. They've left messages every day. The ashes are ready for pickup. I asked them to hold them in storage for three months, but it's been five. Now that the estate has been mostly settled, it's one of the last things on my list. A death list. I wrote it the way I'd write a grocery list; I wrote it the morning after Mother died. I requested that the ashes be packed in a cardboard box for travelling. Now I picture that box sitting on a metal warehouse shelf in the crematorium basement.

"I wonder how many people forget to pick up the ashes?"

"Probably a lot," Diwa says. "We could go get them today."

"I can't. My car's in the shop." Usually Raj handles these maintenance appointments, but now that I've left it feels strange asking him for anything but his patience. "I won't get it back until later tomorrow."

"What about Jyoti? Maybe she could get them."

"Her name isn't on the release."

"Maybe she'd be willing to drive us."

"Doubt it. You know her schedule. She's always busy." I don't want to even bother asking. "We could go the day after tomorrow."

Diwa stares out the window, resolute. "We could take the bus. The number eight goes that way."

"Another day won't make a difference."

"You don't want to go, do you?"

"Who would? It's not something anyone would want to do."

He turns to me. "She's gone. Having Mother's ashes isn't going to make her any more gone."

I look away. "You're right."

Picking up the ashes is a transaction like any other. At the service counter I hand over our invoice to a young woman who barely makes eye contact. Her blond hair is pulled back in a tight bun and she's wearing a blazer whose buttons pull at the chest, undermining what is clearly an attempt to look respectful. She tells us to have a seat and goes off to the back. We wait, sitting quietly on an overstuffed leather sofa, staring at the dated wallpaper border that runs the length of the room. Next to us is an indoor water fountain with a sign that says *Do not touch. For display only.* The sound of water, meant to be of comfort, only makes me anxious. I get up and circle the room. I feel caged and nauseated.

Diwa looks over at me. "Are you okay?"

"Yes." I unzip my jacket. "It's just hot in here." I reach for a paper cup from the water dispenser and pour. "Do you want some?" My voice breaks a bit.

He shakes his head, and after a moment I sit back down. Bereavement literature is fanned across the glass coffee table before us. I pick up a pamphlet titled "Coping with Loss and Grief" and have trouble moving beyond the subtitle, "Someone You Love Has Died."

In the adjacent chapel, a service starts. Double doors open; mourners in black are ushered inside. The priest sees me watching and pulls the heavy doors shut. *Someone they love has died.*

I go back to the glossy pamphlet, turning it over in my hands. A sunset—not so different from the pictures on a travel brochure. Diwa is sitting next to me, his hands folded in his lap, head down. Everything is strangely quiet, tiptoes and whispers. Somewhere I hear someone crying softly. Perhaps they're in the bathing room, holding their dead one last time, just as I did.

Mother's body was lying on a gurney, draped in a white sheet, her long silver hair spilling off the edge of the table like spools of tangled thread. "Mother?" I whispered. Then recognition. Sorrow. "Mother." My head down next to hers. I ran a soft cotton towel across her cold body, lifting her heavy limbs, washing and praying. I shampooed her hair, gently wrung the water out, then combed and twisted it in a style she would have liked. I tried not to think about what I was doing. This was our custom. Before she died she excused me from this duty, suggesting I leave it to the professionals. "Let them do their job. It's better that you not be there." I hadn't known what she meant until that moment. Seeing the dead changes how you experience memory. Everything is final; your grief is weighted with the heaviness that comes with holding up limb and bone. That was all that was left of her. She didn't look like herself anymore, not even when I dressed her in her burial clothes. Her face was waxy, cold, frozen—preserved in its otherness. I looked away as the attendants transferred her from gurney to casket. When she was at rest I had trouble leaving. I stood, holding vigil, for over an hour. I couldn't bring myself to close the lid, to shut her inside such a small dark space.

The nurse at the hospital had said it was normal to want to stay with the dead. "Take all the time you need," she said. "But we do suggest that you not be present when the body is removed." One minute Mother was a person and the next she was a body. When we left that evening, we saw the orderlies go into the room with a gurney and body bag. I wanted to run back and tell them "I need more time."

It's been my mantra ever since. Most days I move through the world unable to comprehend the living. Hating their sure-footedness, their superficiality. Now, it seems, there is just one single truth: our lives are insignificant. There is no great pur-pose, there is just this moment.

When the woman returns with the ashes, I fold the brochure, stuff it in my pocket, and walk to the counter. "The remains are packed in airtight plastic inside the box," she says, explaining that they're ready for transport and shouldn't be transferred to a glass or ceramic urn. "If you do transfer them into another vessel, the x-ray scanner at the airport won't be able to image properly and you won't be able to travel with them."

"Oh." I hadn't thought of any of this.

The woman's demeanour softens. "Believe me, it happens all the time. People have to leave their loved ones behind at airport security and have another family member pick them up. You can imagine how distressing that would be." She hands me a release form. Her pink nail polish is chipped. "Sign and date here," she says, pointing with the tip of her pen. "And here."

"That's it?"

She nods and hands me the cardboard box. I thank her, but it doesn't feel right. I carry the box in both hands, like an offering. Neither Diwa nor I thought to bring a bag. Out in the spring cold we walk the kilometre back to the bus stop and wait for half an hour, watching cars whiz by in the usual going-here-and-there rush. As we get on the bus, I hand Diwa the box and then pay the fare. He walks to the back and we sit down shoulder to shoulder, facing another bank of seats where a grubby man with tattoos sits with his gum-snapping girlfriend. He wraps his arm around her, whispers something in her ear. She tosses her hair and laughs. Behind them the streets are a blur. Diwa too holds the box with both hands, covering the label that says *Human Remains*. "Hold tight," I say. The bus lurches to a stop, passengers thrown forward and backward in a steadying balance. Diwa's knuckles are white. In my pocket I can feel the corners of the grief pamphlet jabbing my thigh. *Someone we love has died.*

THEN

The baby is crying. I know this before my eyes open, before I'm awake, and I wonder if she's crying at all or if my knowing makes it so. Perhaps it's a dream. I wait, and as my eyes adjust to the pre-dawn light I can hear her in her crib fighting off her swaddled blanket, her cries like a kitten meowing in the night, quiet and desperate. My milk lets down. "Fuck," I say out loud, crossing my arms over my breasts to stop the flow. I switch on the lamp and go to her. Sharon is wet, her sheets are wet, her diaper has leaked. "Shit." I pick her up, cradling her in one arm, bouncing and shushing, while pulling off the sheets with the other. I wonder how Raj can sleep through this, but somehow he does and I resent him for it. I drop the sheets into the overflowing hamper and take her to her change table. She cries the whole time, even while I dress her in a clean diaper and sleeper. I move quickly, trying to be delicate, but this moment is like a bomb—take too long and it will explode into hours of overtired wailing. I pick her up and sit in the rocking chair, grabbing the ridiculous C-shaped nursing cushion. She latches on. I sigh in the relief and agony of that momentary clamp of mouth to flesh. As her body relaxes into mine she makes the smallest sounds, murmurs and flutters, a language of her own. When she falls asleep I stoop over the crib, laying her back in tenderly so she won't feel the separation that usually startles her. As I begin to straighten up I see my reflection in the mirror across the room. My hair is pulled back in a messy ponytail, my T-shirt is half up and half down, one breast hanging out of the nursing bra flap, the C-shaped cushion still lodged around my hips. This is motherhood. My body a utility. I clip the nursing bra flap shut and return to bed.

"Everything okay?" Raj asks, his back to mine.

"Yes." He turns and puts his arm around me, resting his hand on my breast. "Don't, that hurts." I move his hand to keep a let-down of milk from rushing.

"Sorry," he says, nuzzling my neck. I pretend not to notice as his body stiffens against mine. I'm not interested in sex. The health nurse said this is normal for some women, especially given the rapid succession of my pregnancies. "It's been only sixteen months since the stillborn." She doesn't call it a baby. Last week she came to the house to check on us. She weighed and measured Sharon and asked me a series of innocuous questions meant to annotate my mental state, which is important, she said, given my most recent history with postpartum. I wondered if it was still considered "postpartum" since the other baby was stillborn. I remembered when I stopped feeling the in-utero movements, the panic on the way to the hospital, the crushing blow of having to deliver this child, the shock of seeing its lifeless premature body. I had carried it for thirty-two weeks, felt its being flutter through mine, absorbed its cells, and yet it never existed. There is no record of it, except the one that is written on my body. Five months later its grave became a womb again. I worried about the new baby. Did Sharon inherit that trauma, did she absorb sadness as if it were nourishment? What is passed from mother to child? I wanted to ask the nurse, but surely that would only be cause for more concern and more visits.

"I just have a few more questions," the health nurse said as she cheerfully checked off boxes and filled in blanks. "Just answer A, B, C, or D, okay?"

I nodded and she began.

1. *I have been able to laugh and see the funny side of things.*
   a. As much as I always could
   b. Not quite so much now
   c. Definitely not so much now
   d. Not at all

"A," I said.

2. *I have looked forward with enjoyment to things.*
   a. As much as I ever did
   b. Rather less than I used to
   c. Definitely less than I used to
   d. Hardly at all

"A again."

·

3. *I have blamed myself unnecessarily when things went wrong.*

    a. Yes, most of the time

    b. Yes, some of the time

    c. Not very often

    d. No, never

"D. It's always my husband's fault." I laughed but she didn't smile; she was focused on her clipboard questions.

4. *I have been anxious or worried for no good reason.*

    a. No, not at all

    b. Hardly ever

    c. Yes, sometimes

    d. Yes, very often

"B."

5. *I have felt scared or panicky for no good reason.*

    a. Yes, quite a lot

    b. Yes, sometimes

    c. No, not much

    d. No, not at all

"A, I mean C."

6. *Things have been getting on top of me.*

    a. Yes, most of the time I haven't been able to cope

    b. Yes, sometimes I haven't been coping as well as usual

    c. No, most of the time I have coped quite well

    d. No, I have been coping as well as ever

"D," I said with the confidence of someone on a roll, a winning streak of TV game show proportion.

7. *I have been so unhappy that I have had difficulty sleeping.*
   a. Yes, most of the time
   b. Yes, sometimes
   c. Not very often
   d. No, not at all

"None of the above."

She stopped, confused. "You have to choose one of the options."

"But I don't sleep because I have a newborn."

"I'll just put D then," she said and smiled.

8. *I have felt sad or miserable.*
   a. Yes, most of the time
   b. Yes, quite often
   c. Not very often
   d. No, not at all

"C. I mean, sometimes I'm sad because I'm tired, but not for any other reason. That's normal, right?"

"Of course it's normal. Now on to question nine."

9. *I have been so unhappy that I have been crying.*
   a. Yes, most of the time
   b. Yes, quite often
   c. Only occasionally
   d. No, never

"I cry all the time, but not because I'm unhappy. Is that normal?"

"Of course," she said. "It's just hormones. But have you been unhappy since the baby was born?"

"Yes, but no, not really?" This was a trick question.

"I'll just put C for once or twice then." She waited for my approval.

"Okay. Is that it?" My afternoon soap opera would be on soon, the only thirty minutes of alone time I'd have all day.

"One last question."

10. *The thought of harming myself has occurred.*
        a. Yes, quite often
        b. Sometimes
        c. Hardly ever
        d. Never

"D, never," I said, offended. "I would never."

"Sorry, I have to ask. It's just part of the survey." She put the questionnaire in her bag. "Before I go, last time you mentioned that breastfeeding wasn't going so well. How's the nursing pillow and the new latching technique? The football hold is usually easiest for new moms."

"It's better. I think I've got the hang of it now. I just thought it would be easier."

"That's a common feeling. People think all aspects of motherhood will be intuitive, but that's not true for every woman. And how are your breasts?"

"Pardon?"

"Are there any cracks or clogs?"

"I don't think so," I said, crossing my arms over my chest, aware that she was looking at them as if they were ductwork or pipes, something to be fixed.

"Would you like me to take a look?"

"Sure, I guess." I lifted up my shirt and unlatched the flaps of my bra.

She put her glasses on and took a close look, cupping each breast. "Sorry for the cold hands," she said and then dropped them. I scooped them back into the cups, pressing and smoothing the bra bulges that come with the spill of double-D breasts.

"Everything looks fine. If you have any difficulty with cracking nipples you can get a cream through your pharmacist." She wrote the name of the cream on a piece of paper and handed it to me. "Any issues with sex?"

"What? No," I said, surprised by the change in topic. "I haven't, we haven't."

"Has your doctor cleared you?"

"Yes. It's not that—it's just, I'm not ready."

"Of course. It's important to listen to your body. You'll know when it's right."

That night in bed, sex was all I thought about. It had been eight weeks since the baby was born. We'd stopped having sex in my last trimester; Raj was worried about the baby and didn't want to take any chances. I wondered whether that was the truth or if it was just my body that turned him off. One evening I'd come home early from my book club and heard him jacking off to hard-core porn. There he was sitting on the couch, a bath towel over his lap, lube on the coffee table, watching two women in dog collars being fucked in the ass. I stood in the door and watched him come, saw the horrified look when he realized I was there. We didn't talk for days. We never spoke of it. And now here he is pressing on my behind, grinding like a sixteen-year-old boy. I reach back and grab his cock as he pulls down my pyjamas. He takes me from behind. I don't feel much more than discomfort, and for him I imagine it's like fucking a pinball machine. He's sticking it in whatever slot works and hearing bells go off, not knowing whether they mean anything. He's saying things; I pretend not to hear his sex talk and just take each hit.

"Do you like it? Do you want it?" He asks this over and over. All I can think of is

> a. No
>
> b. Some of the time
>
> c. Yes
>
> d. All of the time
>
> e. None of the above

It's the ringing phone that wakes her in the middle of the night. Amrita sits up, startled, waiting for something to happen, but nothing does and she lies back down. Moonlight streams in, casting a silver glow. Then Father's voice, at first a low murmur, gets louder. Mattress coils squeak as he gets up and crosses the room. She lies there listening to the floorboards creak, his feet thumping. He is running. She gets up and rushes into the hallway, but he's already outside. She watches from the courtyard as his driver opens the passenger door. They're in the car and down the road before she can call his name. She pads back to her room, her heart full of dread. She doesn't sleep until dawn.

When Amrita wakes, the house is quiet. Servants avoid her. Even Ruby doesn't look at her when she asks whether Pyara has sent any messages today. "No, miss." Amrita's shoulders slump while Ruby clears the breakfast table, set for one.

"Has Father not returned?" Amrita looks at his empty chair.

Ruby shrugs.

"And Dadi ji? I haven't seen her today."

Ruby shrugs again.

"What's wrong with you? You're so quiet today."

Ruby looks down at the tray of dishes she's carrying. "Sorry, miss." She waits to be excused. Amrita listens to the china rattle as Ruby walks out of the room. She stares out the window across the field and then wanders out onto the veranda, waiting for Pyara to pass by. The sight of him, a stolen glance, is always enough, but today he does not pass. Soon it's lunchtime, and then dinner. The house is still quiet. She eats alone, her dinner tray barely touched, her stomach knotted in worry.

It is after ten by the time her father and Dadi ji return home.

"What's happened?" Amrita asks, peppering Dadi ji with questions as she crosses the hallway. She is walking more slowly than usual.

"Not now."

"Why? What's happened?" Amrita follows her upstairs.

Dadi ji collapses on the bed. Her eyes are full; she wipes them with the end of her chunni. Then she stands up and hugs Amrita, her shoulders quaking. "Poor girl," she says and begins to cry.

Amrita stiffens and pulls away. "What's happened?"

Dadi ji looks away, as all the others have.

"Look at me," Amrita demands. "Someone tell me, what is it?"

"An accident," Father says. He's standing in the doorway. "Pyara was in an accident."

"What happened? Is he all right?"

"Last night. In Jalandhar."

"What? What is it? Tell me."

"There was an accident. An oncoming car lost control or the driver fell asleep—the police don't know for sure."

"The police? But what about Pyara? Is it bad?"

"He's conscious now." Father hesitates, glancing at Dadi ji, who nods. "He's out of surgery."

"Surgery? What surgery? Oh my God. He'll be all right then. Can I see him?"

"Amrita, his leg was crushed in the accident. They couldn't save it."

"What? I don't understand. What do you mean, save it?"

"They had to amputate it."

"Take me to him. I want to see him." Amrita makes for the door. "We have to go at once."

"No, child." Dadi ji reaches for her. "That is no place for you."

"But I'm to marry him," she says, as if she's making a point. "There is no better place for me."

Her father looks away, refusing to meet her eyes.

"But, Father," she says, forcing him to meet her gaze. "You said it yourself. The arrangements have been made."

He shakes his head.

"No. You said it's been decided." Amrita closes in on her father. "You can't go back on your word."

He grabs her by the shoulders. "Enough. My daughter won't marry a cripple."

"But, Father!"

"No buts. You heard what I said, didn't you?" He stops, takes a breath, and lets her go. "It's been a long day."

Dadi ji puts her arm around Amrita. "It's late, child; you should sleep."

"How can I?" Amrita pushes Dadi ji's arm away. "How could you do this to me?" She rushes to her room and sits by the window, watching the moon, praying to whatever God will listen.

THEN

It's three in the afternoon and Charles has fallen asleep. The sun streams in through the break in the curtains, one sharp ray illuminating our sordid and calculated afternoon. Clothes draped on the back of a chair, an ice bucket, room-service trays barely touched. I pour myself the last bit of champagne and watch him sleep. He's beautiful. Older than I am but still youthful in the way he moves and wears his hair, slightly longer, more dishevelled than most men in his position. "Boy next door." That's what the nurses call him when he's out of earshot. I've even seen his patients sit up straighter, pinch their cheeks, and check their pocket mirrors when they hear him making his rounds. No matter how sick they are, they seem sunnier when he's at their bedside. "He has a way about him, doesn't he? I wonder if he's single," a patient asked me today.

"Divorced, I think," I said while changing her IV.

We hadn't planned this affair. It was a string of night shifts, reduced staffing, and the kinds of conversations that happen during two a.m. smoke breaks. He smoked, I didn't. "I should really quit" was the first thing he said to me that wasn't about charts and medications.

I nodded.

"You don't smoke?"

"Nope," I said, walking closer to him. "I just come out here to get some air."

"Sorry." He lowered his cigarette to his side.

I reached for his hand, took the cigarette from his fingers, and held it to my lips, inhaling and exhaling slowly. "It's okay," I said, dropping the cigarette to the ground and stepping on it. Then I walked away from him, something inside me smouldering.

I sit on the edge of the bed as I get dressed. He stirs and moves closer. His hand on the small of my back then his mouth on my neck, the scruff of his beard on my shoulders. I close my eyes and let this happen for a moment. His arms around me, his hands undoing buttons, my breath shallow, my mouth on his, the curve of his spine as his body pivots to mine. The weight of him on me, around me. We disappear into a perfect rhythm of eyes closed, mouths open, greedy lovemaking. Now we're on our backs, naked and vulnerable. I reach for the sheets but they're puddled at the edge of the bed. "Leave them," he says. "I want to look at you."

He reaches for his cigarettes and lights one, passing me the first drag. "No, thanks." I get out of bed and head into the washroom. "I thought you were quitting."

"It's a process," he says. "Come back."

"I can't. I have to go." I step into the shower. He's still talking but I can't hear what he's saying over the sound of the water. I strain to make out the words, recognizing only the rhythm of his saying my name. It was this that I loved. The way he said my name was always a surrendering of sorts—an exhale.

When I get out of the shower he's sitting in the armchair, half dressed and shirtless like some kind of movie star. I remember the first time we were together. I loved the heft of his body moving on mine, sinewy muscle so different from Raj's slight frame. When I was with Charles, I could disappear into him, into us—but now that was over.

I sit on the edge of the bed and finish dressing.

"So this is it," he says, still relaxed. His voice floats, never breaks, never rises.

"When do you leave?" I'm buttoning my blouse.

"Day after tomorrow. Movers are coming tonight."

I don't say anything.

"I'll miss you," he says.

I smile. Silence. "We both knew what this was." I'm still convincing myself.

He picks up the champagne bottle and drops it into the bucket of melted ice. "Empty," he says. "And what was it that we both knew it was?"

"That's not fair. You knew I was married."

"Do you love your husband?" He leans forward, his eyes intense.

I pick up my purse and rifle through it, looking for my keys. "Of course I do. What kind of question is that? I thought we weren't going to do this." I sigh. "What about you? Did you love your first wife?" I feel mean for having said it, for making this hard on him when I know his divorce was difficult.

"I did."

"So what happened?"

"I don't know. Life, I guess."

"I guess that's what this is—life."

He doesn't answer and I glance at my watch. "I have to go or I'll be late picking up Sharon."

Saying her name, reminding him that I'm someone's mother, is like a grenade. Charles surrenders. He opens the door. I step out and turn toward him one more time, unsure how to leave.

"Sim, are you happy?"

I kiss his cheek. "You take care."

He watches me until the elevator doors open. As they close behind me I exhale as though I've been holding my breath for too long. At the next floor down a man in a suit steps on. I nod, tight-jawed and perfectly composed.

I'm an hour late. All the other children are gone, abandoned toys littering the front garden of the in-home daycare. Sally is on the front porch when I rush up the steps. "Sorry, sorry. Traffic."

"It's okay," she says, looking at me funny. She points to the buttons on my shirt. "You missed a few."

I look down and quickly pull my trench coat closed. "I spilled coffee on my shirt—had to buy a new one."

Sally opens the door. "She's just inside."

I walk into the cramped foyer and through the narrow house to the back, where a bright yellow wall is full of finger-painted artwork. Sharon is playing Trouble with Sally's own home-schooled kids. "Time to go, Sharon."

She doesn't look up. She pops the dome and makes her move, counting pegs. "Your turn," she says to the little boy with long hair.

"Sharon." I reach for her coat on the chair. "I'm here. It's time to go." I hold her coat the way a matador holds his cape, only she doesn't charge and I'll have to wrestle her in. I draw closer. "Come, we have to get going. We'll grab some dinner on the way home if you like."

She looks up. "I ate already."

Sally jumps in. "I hope you don't mind. She was hungry. It was no trouble."

"Thank you." I wrap the coat around Sharon, drawing one arm through at a time as if I were threading a needle.

"Ouch," she says abruptly, snapping her arm away. "I'll do it myself."

Embarrassed in front of Sally, the home-school hippie, I stand back and wait, watching as Sharon collects her backpack. When she lets Sally help her with her zipper, I have to look away.

"See you tomorrow," Sharon says, waving to the boys before hugging Sally around the hips. Sally pats her on the head and pulls back from the embrace, smiling awkwardly.

"She's a great kid," she says as we turn to leave.

"I know." I don't look back.

Raj and I pull into the driveway at the same time. He gets out of the car with a big bag of Chinese food. "Sally called, so I knew you were late. Thought I'd grab your favourite."

"Thanks," I say as we walk into the house.

Sharon goes straight to her room and shuts the door.

"What's that about?" Raj asks.

"She's just mad that I was late or maybe that I showed up at all. I'm not sure which. I tried to talk to her on the way home, but she gave me the silent treatment. Can you believe that?" I pull out dinner plates from the cupboard. "I would never have done that when I was her age. My mother would have smacked me."

"No kidding. Times have changed."

"Still, she's too young to have this much attitude."

Raj grabs the wine glasses and pours me a glass of red. "It sounds like you need this," he says. "Sharon, dinner," he shouts.

"I already ate," she yells from the top of the stairs. "Pork chops."

He looks over at me.

"She was playing Trouble when I got there. Didn't want to leave."

He nods and I see in his eyes that he understands. He puts his hand on my back as I dole out the sweet and sour pork, fried rice, and vegetables—combo number 3—onto our plates. "Lots of people work and have kids. It's not supposed to be this hard, is it?" I ask.

"I wish I knew." He pauses. "I'll be right back. I have an idea." He rushes down the basement stairs and returns a few minutes later with a stack of board games. He dusts off Trouble. "It's the original set," he says as he sets up the pegs. "What colour do you want to be?" He asks this loud enough for Sharon to hear.

"Red," I say, choosing her favourite colour. I hear her gasp.

As we settle into our meal, every so often he presses the Pop-O-Matic dome and counts down spaces. We laugh, pretending to play, until finally she bounds into the room.

"I want to play too! But I get to be red," she declares, sliding into the chair next to me. She grabs my fortune cookie and cracks it open. I wink at her and she smiles.

"All right," Raj says. "New game. Help me set up the board."

She moves all the pegs to the starting position. Raj smiles and we clink glasses. To a new start, I think to myself.

Mother isn't speaking to me anymore.

Not since the ashes came home last week. I ask her if she's angry with me, but there's no answer. For the first time since she died, she's gone.

When we brought the ashes home, I didn't know where to put them. At first I placed them on the mantel, but every time I walked into the living room I felt uneasy, worried that the box would fall and Mother would spill onto the carpet. I imagined guests innocently asking, "What's in the box?," my replying, "Mother," and then their look of horror. So I decided *no*—ashes are not a decorative object, not a candelabra or a cuckoo clock. Ashes are meant to be scattered, not displayed. In the meantime I cleared off the top shelf of my bedroom closet and set her there. Every morning since, I've looked up at that box, reconciling myself to its contents and Mother's silence.

She's gone, replaced by ashes.

I stare at the box, thinking how easy it would be to tuck it away and forget about it. Years ago there was a story on the local news about a sealed urn ending up in a thrift shop. The woman who bought it thought it was an antique Chinese vase. She took it home and set the blue-and-white porcelain urn on the coffee table, unaware of its contents until her Siamese cat knocked it over and used the ashes as litter. It turned out that the urn had been donated by the new owners of a historic home—they'd found it in the garage with many other items and had donated them all, not realizing that the urn held someone's loved one. After the story aired, relatives of the original homeowners came forward to claim what remained of their great-grandfather. At the time, Mother and I had a good laugh about the "buyer beware" story. Recalling it now only makes me want to cry.

The doorbell rings and I can hear Diwa get up to answer it. It must be Jyoti, here so that we can decide what to do next.

I grab a step stool and climb up to retrieve the box. I cradle it close to my chest as I take it into the kitchen, where Diwa and Jyoti are sitting.

"Wow, you look a mess," Jyoti says.

"I haven't been feeling well." Glancing at her nautical designer outfit that makes her look as if she's going to the yacht club, I place the box on the kitchen table and sit down. The fluorescent tubes in the ceiling light flicker, casting a waxy glow.

"So, what are we supposed to do with them?" Jyoti asks.

"I'm not sure. Mother didn't leave instructions." It's quiet except for the hum of the refrigerator. The sound reminds me of the hospital's mechanized apparatus, the constant backdrop and curtain fall of our questions. What to do next?

Diwa sits quietly at the end of the table, in Mother's favourite spot. He's writing something but I don't know what. I've realized that sometimes he writes just to avoid the awkward silences and eye contacts of everyday life. His glasses are at the edge of his nose and he pushes them up periodically.

"I don't know why you bothered bringing them back, then," Jyoti says. "We could have interred them in the columbarium on site. It would have been way less hassle."

"Hassle?" I don't even try hiding my frustration. "Is that what you think this is?"

"That's not what I mean. I just mean we could have buried them or something."

"No, we couldn't. We can't," Diwa says. "Ashes have to be scattered in flowing water." He looks up at us over his glasses professorially. "Mother told me so."

"Of course she did."

"Jyoti, please." I want to avoid an argument.

Diwa has cowered into himself, just as he did when he was little and the white coats asked about his remembering.

"Fine. If not a columbarium, what do you suggest?" Jyoti taps her manicured nails on the table and raises her eyebrows, although the expression is barely discernible on her Botoxed face.

"The ashes have to be scattered in water that flows," Diwa says again. "A river or stream, any body of water that connects to the ocean."

"What about India?" I ask. "We could take her back home."

"What? This *is* her home. I don't think Mother expected us to go all the way to India," Jyoti says.

"I know, but you've never been—and if ever there was a time for us to go together, it seems this would be it."

"You're suggesting we take the ashes there?" Diwa asks.

I nod, the thought of it growing in my mind. "Sure, why not? We could see where Mother grew up. The land and farm, it's all still there, and it's ours now. We're the only family left."

"I'm not so sure it's a good idea," Diwa says.

"But we're going to have to decide what to do with the land— whether we should sell it or keep leasing it out. We may as well go and see it."

"I'm with Diwa on this," Jyoti says, shaking her head. "Going to India isn't an easy thing—we can't just pick up and go like it's Vegas or something. We'd have to get visas, get shots, and figure out how to navigate our way once we've arrived. We don't know anyone there. The country is completely corrupt. Besides, I don't know if I could swing it. The kids' schedules are so hectic right now, and Nikhil has been super busy and stressed at work. It's terrible timing." She checks her watch and then stands up. "Speaking of which, I have to get going."

"Timing? Seriously?"

"Stop it. Just stop," Diwa says. "Have you forgotten why we're here?"

"You're right." I'm still glaring at Jyoti. "Look, I don't expect going to India to be easy, but I think we owe it to her to try to do this one last thing right. Lord knows we did everything else wrong."

"Speak for yourself, Simran," Jyoti says. "I didn't do anything wrong. I don't share your guilt."

"Well, you should." I get up and thrust the box of ashes into her arms. "You were hardly the picture-perfect daughter. Once you snagged a rich husband you couldn't get out of here fast enough."

"How dare you? You don't know anything about me." Jyoti

tries to push the box toward me but I shove it right back, pressing it to her chest.

"Take it. For once, *you* accept some responsibility for this family."

"Cut it out," Diwa says, still trying to intervene.

Jyoti shoves the box at me again, but I step back and it falls. The vacuum-packed remains tumble out.

We edge away, staring at the ashes, not sure what to do. Mother is on the floor.

"Now see what you've done." Jyoti kneels down to put the bag back in the box. She stares at the ash and shards of bone through the sealed plastic, holding the box in her arms like a newborn. She's crying. Diwa looks on, bewildered, and together we watch her gently place the box back on the table.

Neither of us says anything.

"It's like I didn't even exist." Jyoti is drying her eyes with her sleeve as she sits back down at the table. "I was just there, you know. My whole life, until I got married, I was just there." She's looking up at me now.

"I know. We all were. You, me, Diwa—all of us. Sometimes I think we were waiting for something to happen, and then nothing did." I sit down, rocked by my own realization, listening to the clocks tick. "Mother used to call it the *what's next life* . . . she'd once heard some teenage girls talking on the bus and had imitated them: *And then this happened, and then that happened . . . And then and then.*" I smile at the recollection of her voice, her tone, so matter-of-fact and undaunted.

"And then—this." Jyoti glances at the box of ashes, her eyes welling up.

Diwa hands her his handkerchief. "I'm sorry," Jyoti says and blows her nose. "I just, I'm not good at this. I don't know what

I'm supposed to do. Mother always seemed to go to you or Diwa. I just thought you'd take care of everything."

"Is that what you want?"

Jyoti turns to face me. "Yes. Is that bad?"

I hug her, both of us softening into the awkwardness of the rare embrace. "I know it's hard, but we have to do this together."

Jyoti nods and pulls away. "And what about all that?" She's looking over at the overstuffed living room, the wall curios, the collectibles. "When are we going to find time to deal with it?" She walks into the room and picks up one of Mother's blue-and-white porcelain figurines. "She has dozens of these in the basement. She thought they were genuine." Jyoti turns it over. "Made in China." She laughs. A cuckoo clock chimes and then bells sound all over the house, alerting the hour in every room, a few seconds apart. "How do you live with that?" she asks Diwa.

"You get used to it."

"Yeah, I suppose I've just forgotten." The cuckoos fall silent. Now just the ticking of clocks again.

"She liked the sound. She liked all of this," Diwa says.

"Father made her stop collecting for a while, but after he died she started right up again," I say. "She'd ask me to check the classifieds and help map out her round of yard sales. Never the estate sales, though."

"Why not?"

"She thought it was disrespectful. We tried once, you know. I took her to this gorgeous place in the west end, a grand old Tudor with a rose garden out back. There were antiques and furs and clothes—Jyoti, you would have loved it—but Mother wouldn't look through any of it. She just wandered through the house, staring at the dirt marks where framed pictures used to hang, the great hall and the chandeliers, the oak staircase and inlaid walls. Scavengers, she called them—all the people taking the house apart piece by piece. She was so upset when I told her later that it had finally been sold and all its history dismantled. Even the roses were dug up. Then the house was demolished to make room for a new build."

Jyoti paused, considering. "So what do you think she'd want us to do with her things?"

"Definitely not an estate sale." I flop onto the sofa, surveying the room. "But we'll have to go through it all eventually."

"Where to start?"

"We go room by room, figuring out what to keep and what to give away. We can keep track in a log or put colour-coded stickers on everything." The weight of death's most practical details suddenly fills me with guilt. "It won't be easy."

Jyoti picks through a box of mismatched picture frames, some still with the stock pictures that came with them, others with family photographs. "She sure held on to a lot of stuff," she says, handing me a black-and-white photo. "I don't even know who this person is."

It's a picture of Pyara.

Diwa looks over my shoulder at the photo, showing no sign of recognition. He's forgotten. I'm alone in my knowledge of the past.

I place the frame back in the box. "You're right. She did hold on to a lot of things."

THEN

The phone rings in the middle of the night, slicing the night into two pieces—before and after. I sit up instantly, intuitively, wondering if I'd sat up before the phone even rang. I'm filled with dread. Raj reaches over in the darkness and answers the call. I switch on the bedside lamp and anxiously listen to his one-sided talk.

"Hello . . . Yes . . . What?"

He bolts upright and flings his legs over the bed, his back to me. I get out of bed and pace the length of the room.

"Wait, wait, slow down . . . You're not making sense . . . When? . . . Don't go anywhere, I'll be right over."

He hangs up the phone. "It's your father. He's missing."

"What do you mean *missing*?"

"He must have wandered away. That was Jyoti on the phone. They've called the police already. I'm going over."

"I don't understand. How could they let this happen?"

"I'll know more once I get there. All I know is that your mother said he wasn't in bed when she woke up, and that when she went to find him, the front door was wide open. That's when she woke Jyoti to call the police." He rummages through his dresser drawers. "Have you seen my blue sweatshirt?"

I pull it out of the bottom drawer and hand it to him. "What, so they think he just got up and walked away?" I imagine Father wandering the night streets in his robe and slippers. He's wandered before, but never at night and never far from home. I remember once finding him walking toward the temple. When I stopped him, he thought I was Mother—he folded his hands together and lowered his head, saying, "Amrita, take me to Pyara. Forgive me. It wasn't my fault. I tried to tell them. Please, Amrita, take me to Pyara." I put my arm around his shoulders, said that I forgave him, and then took him home to Mother. When I told her what he'd been saying, her eyes sank. "I do forgive him," she said.

Raj runs down the stairs. "Don't worry, I'll call you when I get there."

"Wait, I should come too." I grab my robe and rush after him. "I'll wake Sharon. We'll all go."

Raj stops at the door. "Sim, no. Stay here. She's still sleeping and there's no need to wake her."

I think of her asleep and safe in her bed. "You're right, of course. Call me then." I watch him leave, shutting the door behind him. Then I sit on the bottom step, listening to the quiet of the house, listening to the rain, paying attention to all my fears that gather in the dark. It's just like the night Mother phoned to tell me that Diwa was missing. I was nineteen, living away from home, hungover and in bed with a guy I'd just met. I'd brought him home from a party; we'd done a line together, drunk a bottle of wine, and fucked like mad. The call was sobering. I woke the near stranger, telling him what happened and that I had to go. I got dressed, packed a bag, and the stranger, whose name was Todd, drove me to the Greyhound station and kissed me goodbye. He kissed me like I was someone, like it mattered. I dropped out of school for the semester and spent the next three months looking for Diwa. I made copies of his photograph and tacked them on phone poles and bus stops. I handed out flyers, shoving them in people's faces as they came out of shopping malls and train stations. "Have you seen this boy? Have you seen my brother?" Sometimes people stopped and listened to my story, most times they took the flyer out of pity and stuffed it in their bag, but occasionally they would push by me or else take the flyer, glance at it, and then scrunch it up and throw it in the trash. I once set out to collect all the crumpled ones from the garbage bins. Then I sat down on a park bench, smoothing the creases from Diwa's face while a stack of flyers spilled from my bag and scattered in the wind. By the time I noticed, dozens of sheets were flying and tumbling through the air. I gave chase but couldn't retrieve them all. Eventually I sat down and watched them float away. That's when I met Raj. He sat next to me and asked if I was okay.

I turn on all the lights in the house and open the drapes and blinds; from the street, it must seem as if we're holding vigil. I check on Sharon. She's sprawled out on her stomach, hugging a pillow, sighing and mumbling in a deep teenage sleep. I lean in close, pull up her sheets, and kiss her head.

Raj calls to tell me that a police report has been filed.

"Have they started a search? Where are they looking? Have they talked to the neighbours? Do they know what he was wearing? Do they have a picture? Do they know about his dementia?"

He answers yes to everything. I'm only partly reassured.

"I'm going out with Jyoti; she and I will drive around to see if we can find him. I don't think he could have gotten far."

"Okay, that's good . . . I'll wait for your call."

I hang up and sit in front of the computer. When I search "dementia, missing people," countless websites come up. I click through them, snatching bits of information, headlines. *Six in ten dementia patients will wander. Routines stop wandering. Make your home safe for vulnerable adults. Avoid busy or confusing places like shopping malls. What to do when your loved one goes missing.* Nothing helps. I search "missing person" and scroll through countless pages of names and photos of those who've disappeared. I wonder if they've been found or if they just vanished the way Diwa did. I stare at them and they stare back. Finally I turn off the computer and sit on the couch, my eyes shut. I fall asleep and dream. Father is walking down the dark street in his robe and slippers. It's raining and he's drifting, blown about by the wind, but he's pushing into it, leaning and charging headfirst, covering his face with his arm. In the distance a man holds an umbrella under a moonless slice of sky, stars orbiting above. Father tries to shout to him but no sound comes out of his mouth. Suddenly the dream is quiet, the rain is mist, the wind is trailing smoke. Clouds move and an indigo sky opens. The man under the umbrella approaches; with each step he grows younger until he stands in front of Father as a boy. The boy folds his umbrella, sits on the ground, then takes cars out of his bag and lines them up. Father crouches down and sits with him until the light pours in and flushes out the night.

Raj nudges my shoulder, pulling me from sleep. "What time is it?" I squint; sunlight is crashing through the windows. Raj draws down the blinds.

"It's seven."

"Did you find him?"

He shakes his head. "Not yet. But the police are still out looking."

"How's Mother?" I grab his arm as if it were a lifeline.

"She's okay." He sits down next to me.

"And Jyoti? How's she taking it?"

"She's as freaked out as any twentysomething kid would be, but she's trying."

"Do you think we should tell Sharon?"

"No, let's not say anything yet." He pauses as if searching for the best way to say something. "Let's not tell her anything until there's something to tell."

I understand that he's preparing for the worst.

"Okay, I'll drop her off at school and then go to Mother's. You should shower and sleep."

"It'll be all right." He hugs me and I stay inside his embrace.

Three days later a jogger finds Father's clothes by the riverbank fifteen kilometres from home. Search-and-rescue vessels are deployed. Divers search the black waters but find nothing, no trace of him. I stand with Mother and Jyoti, watching from the shore. Jyoti holds her prayer books and Mother holds my hand. Raj stays at home with Sharon. There is no media attention, no social services; Father is old and our story is sad in a regular way.

Father is presumed dead. His body is never found. Every time I cross the river on my way to work, I imagine it. Somewhere beneath me, beneath the snarl of bridge-deck traffic, the bumper-to-bumper workday grind, he is face down, bloated and blue, floating toward open water. Somewhere beneath me he is tangled up, tied in the drift and weed of cold dark waters.

Pyara is a cripple.

For weeks Amrita begs her father to let her go to him, but he refuses. "It is decided."

"But, Father . . ."

She doesn't finish the sentence. It's pointless. He's already begun the search for a new husband. Everyone in the village knows this. She must marry quickly now. She's been seen with Pyara and must distance the family from the shame. "It was bad enough that he was lower than us, but what use is a one-legged husband for our Amrita?" she heard Dadi ji say to Father. Thus begins the parade of suitors coming through the house. Each day Amrita is forced to present herself to a new possibility; she has no say in the matter. And so she plays along, answering their questions with just a yes or no. But what she says matters little. She is beautiful and fair-skinned and her father can provide a handsome dowry. An offer is made from a family from New Delhi. Dadi ji knows of this family from a friend in a neighbouring village. Their son lives and works in the city. "He has a good job," she explains to Father over tea. "And it would do her good to get away from the village."

"They are asking for too much," he says. "This isn't 1940. I will not pay for someone to marry my daughter."

"It's not payment. It's tradition."

"Tradition is not bars of gold and new cars. This is ridiculous. Tell them that I will not accept the offer. My daughter will not be subject to such backward thinking."

"But, son, any other offer will be the same. People know about Amrita and the boy."

"Whatever they think they know, they are wrong. Refuse the offer."

When Dadi ji sees Amrita smiling about this outcome, she reminds her that there is nothing to smile about. "The only way to restore our honour is a good marriage, understand?"

Amrita nods and is excused to her room, where she's spent most of her time since Pyara's accident. When Ruby comes in with her clean laundry, Amrita presses her for information about Pyara. She's heard the servants talking in the kitchen, their low voices and their laughter—a sure sign of gossip.

"I don't know anything."

"But you've seen him."

"Only when I pass by their gates. He is usually sitting on his cot, reading books. The others say that's all he does: sit and read, read and sit."

"How does he seem?"

"I don't know, miss. The other servants say that he's quiet and keeps to himself. He doesn't want their help and manages most things on his own."

Amrita imagines him hobbling on his one leg, hunched over on his crutches, and it breaks her. "Take a message to him for me," she whispers. "Please."

Ruby nods and Amrita writes out a few lines of Rumi, nothing too telling should she be found out. She presses the note into Ruby's hand. "He mustn't think I've forgotten him."

"Yes, miss." Ruby tucks the note into her basket.

Though two weeks pass without any reply, Amrita writes him each day. She slips the notes under her teacup for Ruby to deliver. Today, Ruby tilts her head, see-saw-like, escaping blame or knowing. "Sorry, miss," she says after breakfast.

"She needn't be sorry," Dadi ji says as she enters the room. "It's not her fault, is it? Ruby, you can go now." Ruby hastily gathers the dirty dishes and darts out of the room.

"What's going on?" Amrita asks. Dadi ji unlocks the desk drawer and retrieves a stack of Amrita's notes. She places them on the table and then sits in the armchair by the morning fire.

"What did you think was going to happen?" Dadi ji doesn't leave time for a response. "Did you think no one would find out?"

"How long have you known?"

"Almost since the first." Dadi ji stamps her cane for effect. "And you should be glad it was me who found out and not your father."

Amrita should feel shame, but she doesn't. "Did he get *any* of them?"

"One." Dadi ji holds up his reply.

Amrita lunges forward, snatching it from her and tearing it open. Her eyes dart across the page. *Rumi says, Love holds everything together and is the everything. And so, my dear Amrita, I have everything . . .*

Dadi ji grabs the note from her before she can finish reading it. "Enough, child, this ridiculousness must end." She crumples it up before tossing it into the fire.

"No!" Amrita rushes to retrieve it.

Dadi ji pushes her back with her cane. "Stop, you'll burn yourself." Then she throws the rest of the notes into the fire.

Amrita watches the poem turn to kindling, charred edges, golden sparks, ash.

"Let this be the end of it," Dadi ji says. "Don't make me tell your father."

The following day Father summons Amrita to his study. "Arrangements have been made," he says, barely looking up from his ledger where he's adding and subtracting his wealth. "You will marry Pyara's brother, Manohor."

"But I thought—"

"Never mind what you thought. Whatever you've done, you've ruined your chances of making a match elsewhere. I've spoken to the family. In his condition, Pyara cannot go abroad, he cannot work. He will stay in India where he can be cared for, and his brother—he will go abroad in his place."

"But, Father—"

He silences her with a look. "Enough, Amrita. I didn't educate you so that you could stay here and care for a cripple. And you'd have no children—what kind of life would that be?"

She knew he wasn't really asking.

"As I said—" He clears his throat. "The arrangements have been made. You will marry in a month. Both families are in agreement. It's the right thing to do. The only thing to do given the circumstances."

In the hallway, Dadi ji doesn't hide her eavesdropping. "It's for the best," she says as Amrita walks out the front door and through the courtyard gate. Her dadi ji is calling, shaking her cane, but Amrita walks on through the mustard fields, toward the banyan tree, where she sits among the twist of roots and branches.

I inhale. The smell of spring and newly cut grass fills the air. Blossoms rain down from the cherry trees lining the street: the world is pink. It seems hard to believe that anything could ever be wrong. I search through my purse for my house key, finally emptying the contents on the front stoop and kneeling down to sort through it all. The door opens. "You could have just rung the bell," Raj says.

I look up. "I didn't know you'd be home." I gather my belongings, stuffing them back into my bag, and follow him into the house. Light fills the living room. There are fresh-cut flowers in a vase on the coffee table next to a neatly stacked pile of magazines. "The place looks great."

"You sound surprised."

"No, not surprised. You always did like a neat house. I just figured you'd be too busy at work to keep up with it. That's all."

"Truth is, I hired a housekeeper. She comes in once a week. I realize now that we should have hired someone years ago."

"Imagine all the arguments we would have avoided." I'm remembering how critical he was of my domestic skills.

"You want coffee? I just made it."

"Sure." I sit down while he goes into the kitchen, feeling like a guest in my own home. I hear the TV in the other room. "Are you watching *Jerry Springer*?"

"Yeah, background noise. Otherwise the house is too quiet," he says, returning with coffee. "Cream and sugar, just the way you like it."

"Mother used to watch it too, for the same reason. Only I'm pretty sure she liked the entertainment factor."

"Don't we all." He sits down across from me on the opposite sofa. "Always nice to know there are people way worse off than you."

I laugh a little, trying to fill the awkward silence.

"This is nice," he says. "Sitting here with you."

I smile and look away when our eyes meet. I'm not sure how to be in this space where we're not husband and wife and yet we are. I take a sip of coffee. "It's good."

"Glad you like it."

The phone rings.

"Excuse me," Raj says, and again I feel like a guest. I listen to him answer, his voice softening in recognition. "It's Sharon," he says, covering the receiver. "Yeah, your mom is here . . . Yeah, everything's fine, she's just here to get a few things for the trip . . . Did you want to talk to her?" He turns his back to me for a moment. "Just talk to her," he says and then thrusts the phone into my hand. "She wants to say hi."

I nod. "Hi, honey."

"Hey, Mom."

"Everything okay at school?"

"Yep. You ready for your trip?"

"Almost—I just came by to pick up my luggage."

"Well, I hope you have a great trip or you know what I mean."

"Yeah, thanks."

"Um, can I talk to Dad?"

"Sure, sweetie." I pass the phone back to Raj and he takes it into the other room.

"I'll just be a few minutes," he says, shutting the door before I can say anything more. I can hear him talking but can make out only a few words: *fine, love, mother* . . . then silence . . . *I understand . . . honey* . . . I suspect she hates me, and that maybe he does too, and that they're talking about their shared disdain, love, and confused affection for me. I want to pick up an extension and listen in the way my own mother would listen in on my conversations with boys, but there is no receiver to hijack and so I settle for conjecture. As I wait, I wander around the room and inspect the artifacts of our life. Photos in silver frames, art objects—all perfectly designed, coordinated, and unoriginal. I'm holding a pewter pear when Raj comes back in. "What was I thinking?"

"You said it."

"She doesn't want to talk to me. You shouldn't have made her."

"No, she doesn't, and yes, I should. She can't go through life thinking she can do whatever she wants."

"She can't?"

"Not when it's disrespectful to others."

"She has a right to be angry with me."

"She does. But that doesn't mean she can't be kind."

I stand at the window and slide it open. A breeze rushes in and the sheers billow and settle around me. "You are so good," I say, turning around. "You've always been better than me."

"I'm not better."

"See, you are so. I've been horrible, and here you are . . ."

"Here I am," he says, and we both pause in our own uncertainty. "I've pulled your suitcase out of the crawl space for you. It's upstairs."

"Thanks, and thank you for your help with arranging everything."

"No problem. I called my uncle in India and he's arranged for a driver to pick you up and take you to your mother's house. I'll email you the details."

"I appreciate it. I can't tell you how freaked out Jyoti is about travelling unescorted."

"I don't blame her. You have to be careful."

"We will." I pause, feeling awkward. "I guess I'll just grab the suitcase and a few things."

Upstairs in our room I lie down, starfish-like, on the king-size bed, resisting the urge to crawl inside the plush covering. I close my eyes, remembering when Sharon was little and we three would lie side by side and still have room left over. I stay there for a few minutes before getting up.

"I also pulled out your toiletry bag," Raj calls from downstairs. "It's in the ensuite."

"Thanks," I say and walk into the closet. I run my fingers along his row of suits, perfectly lined up, colour-blocked and still smelling like cologne. I bury my face in one of his cashmere sweaters and inhale. Then I unzip my suitcase and throw the sweater inside along with my clothes and toiletries.

I pull the suitcase down the stairs, clunking down each step.

"So that's it. You've got everything?"

"Yeah, I think so." I stand there, unsure whether I should hug him or shake his hand. Everything feels formal.

"Okay then." He grabs my suitcase and takes it out to the car. We say a quick goodbye. As I start the car, he knocks on the window. I slide it down and he leans in. "Look, I don't want to rush you, but when you get back, I'd like it if you'd think about coming home."

I pause, taken aback. "I don't know what that would be like," I say.

"Neither do I, not really. Maybe that's the point?" He backs away, waving goodbye with one hand in the air as if to say "I'm here."

THEN

Mother is in the backyard. She's standing in her cotton housecoat with the eastern sun on her back, watering the flowerbeds. It was months after Diwa disappeared that I first saw her here at dawn, digging up earth, placing the poem jar deep in the ground. Around the jar she planted bulbs—tulips, daffodils, hyacinths, crocuses—and each spring since then the flowers have signalled all the beauty that is hidden, a reminder of what still needs to be unearthed.

When I call out to her she waves me over. I tiptoe into the garden so that my heels don't sink into the grass and then teeter toward her. "You wanted to see me?"

She motions to the garden bench. "Sit. I'll just be a minute." As I watch her among her flowers, pulling up weeds, turning soil, I picture life's equilibrium, how seasons blend. Mother is mouthing words. When I ask her what she's saying she becomes flustered, flush with spring and memory, and says it's nothing. But I know it must be his words, his poems. Those scraps she made into a garden, blooming and dying every season. The push of life.

After Father died she started talking about finding Diwa. "I want my life back before it's too late," she said. "I want everything that was taken from me." And now, since her diagnosis, she's been talking about it again. His name, long unuttered, has become commonplace. She sits down next to me. She's frail, her breath laboured. "It's time for Diwa to come home," she says, her eyes tunnelling through mine. "I asked you here because I need your help."

"Mother, we've been through this already."

"I know, but—"

"But what? I wouldn't even know where to begin."

She turns her whole body toward me. "I know that what I'm asking isn't fair. It's hard on you, and I wouldn't ask it if I didn't need it."

"It's been so long. Do you ever think maybe it's better the way things are? Maybe it's better that we just keep moving on?"

"Moving on? Is that what we've been doing?" She stares out at the flowers and shakes her head. "None of us ever moved on. All we did was endure. All I taught you was how to endure life, the things that happened to you. Aren't you tired of that?"

I realize now that everything I thought I'd hidden—my unhappiness, my small defeats, my shrinking world—was always visible to her.

"Simran, I'm dying. There is no moving on for me without this."

"So what is it you want me to do?"

She reaches for my hand and leans in as if she's telling a secret. "I found him."

"What are you talking about?"

She smiles. "Follow me."

With slow, measured steps she walks into the house and up to her room. I sit on the bed as she leans down in front of the dresser. From its bottom drawer she pulls out an accordion file folder. "I hired an investigator I saw on a TV commercial," she says proudly. "To find Diwa, to follow him." She pats the folder. "This is everything you'll need to bring him back. Will you help me?"

I reach for the file, gazing at her in disbelief as I struggle to absorb what she's saying. "What if the information is wrong?" I say finally. "Or what if he doesn't want to come back? I don't want you to get your hopes up."

"What's life without hope, hm? Besides, he'll come back. He always listened to you."

I nod, remembering though that Diwa didn't listen to me the last time we spoke. I'd asked him to come home and he refused. I wonder why it would be different this time.

I drive home with the file on the front seat beside me. No one has seen Diwa in years. But I've thought about him every day, even when I've tried not to. I've recognized him in day-to-day details, in quiet moments and faraway looks, in the faces of strangers. Whenever the seasons changed and natural wonder and drama filled the skies I've wondered what he's thinking. And yet I couldn't possibly know. Twenty-four years have passed. I remember him as a sad, lonely boy in a red windbreaker and pants that were always an inch too short because he outgrew everything so quickly. I remember him one way when surely he is now an entirely different way. This is what happens. The past is always changed by the present. There is no true account, not even the number of years that have gone by. It's what the years hide, reveal, and keep secret, what they tuck into days and minutes, what they fold and slip into dreams and nightmares—that is where the real living is.

A week after Mother gave me the file, I summon the courage to open it.

It's mostly addresses and photos. As I flip through them, decades fall into place. Diwa has grown into a man. Yet his face is still quiet, his expression distant, lost but content.

I call Mother. She tells me she followed Diwa for years before losing his trail. She never told Father, afraid he might send him away again. In all those years she never spoke to Diwa, never mailed him a letter. Occasionally she would watch him from a distance, frequenting the same coffee shops or restaurants, ordering whatever he ordered, sitting just close enough to keep a watchful eye on him.

"How did you keep yourself from saying anything?" I ask.

"I knew it wasn't the right time."

I drive into the east end where he lives, roam the neighbourhood, scan the residents. Drug-addicted clusters, welfare lines, hard-luck cases. Abusive parents, abused children, the unwanted, the unwantable. Brick-and-clapboard buildings, narrow alleys, dumpster diving, hookers, whores, open mouths, open hands, secondhand clothes, cracked shoes, broken soles, old souls, used up, compressed. This is where my brother lives. He lives among the denizens but isn't one of them. He goes about almost unseen. No one interferes with him, no one speaks to him. He has no friends, no foes. He lives in a single-room occupancy hotel where the residents are immigrants, addicts, the elderly, the infirm. The hotel smells of boiled fish and sweat. Day and night the rooms are filled with sounds of the street, of the creatures who roam and want and wait and hope and live and die.

It takes me three attempts before I have the courage to seek him out.

The stairwell is narrow and empty. People keep to themselves. I climb with tentative steps, leaning into the banister, careful not to touch it. On the fifth floor the air is humid, heavy with marijuana and decay. I knock on his door but it swings open. He is sitting, back toward me, at a desk in front of the window. There is a single red geranium on the ledge and the colour, the purpose, the contrast surprises me. He does not turn when I call his name. His hair, curly and unkempt, grazes his shoulders and I suddenly remember his boyhood. He is running, thick-grinned, away from the setting sun into Mother's arms. She whispers something in his ear and musses his curls and he stares at me with his surprising grey eyes that are as round as riverbed stones. I know I've witnessed small mysteries. They come back to me now as hope. I fidget, shuffle, lips twitching, looking for the next word, the right thing, trying to remember how to move from then to now. "I've come for you," I say. "Mother is ill." He does not move. "She's dying."

He looks up from his book. I see his reflection in the dirty window and am struck with his raw beauty. I've never known a man to look beautiful; the sight of my brother grown up into this lovely stranger moves me. I pause. "She's asked for you."

He stands up and turns toward me but still there is no embrace, only remembrance. I can tell by his eyes that he too is calculating the years lost. I expect him to say something, to ask about Mother, but he doesn't.

"You cut your hair," I say.

"I did. You were right. It helps to blend in."

He turns again, opens an armoire, and begins to pile his belongings into an old suitcase. His clothing is creased and worn—linen suit, suspenders, relics from a time gone by. He packs meticulously. I notice he barely limps anymore.

"How long does she have?" His back is to me.

"It could be months, years, if she's lucky."

He folds and rolls and repacks. "Where will I stay?" His voice, like a chord, reverberates, shadows and echoes inside each word.

"With Mother or with me and Raj, if you prefer. We have space; you can use Sharon's room."

"Sharon?"

"My daughter. She's away at university." I hear my own words and suddenly years of living fall into a void, a wasteland.

"And Raj is your husband?"

"Yes."

"Do you have other children?"

"No, just the one." I stare out the window. There is a police car, lights flashing but no siren. People have gathered. "I had another child, but he died before he was born."

"I'm sorry." Diwa finishes his packing in silence. I watch him, slowly taking stock, integrating the features of this man into my understanding of my brother. He has the same expression, a face full of wonder. I can tell that as he looks at the world he's still indexing, making order out of everything around him, just as he did when he was younger. After he ran away I found his collections at Bibi Jeet's farm. He'd gathered rocks and stamps, compiled books of pressed flowers and butterflies. Wings and petals, frayed and pressed between wax paper. But no poems.

I wonder if he remembers.

NOW

Jyoti is asleep, her head bobbing on my shoulder. She's taken a sleeping pill, chased it with vodka, and has been out for most of the flight, waking up for only a few groggy minutes at a time. Diwa sits across the aisle, his head resting against the window, staring out into the black of night. I tried to sleep but the rattle and quake of engines and turbulence kept waking me. My ears are plugged, dampened like the whirling inside a seashell. I glance at my carry-on bag tucked under the seat in front of me and resist the urge to check the ashes again. For a week I've had a recurring dream that I'd forgotten them, that I'd abandoned Mother in a box on the closet shelf; I rush home and find her sitting on the couch, alive, waiting for us. This morning I checked my carry-on a dozen times before we left, just to be sure, and each time I was somehow disappointed that there she was, just ash—not waiting. Around me the cabin sleeps, except for a few passengers, their overhead lights shining down like sentinels across the rows. I watch the transatlantic flight path on the seatback screen, below us only water, and try not to think of Malaysian Airlines Flight 370. But the more I reject the idea the more I think of them, row upon row of missing and presumed dead, now somewhere beneath us in watery graves. "Don't worry," Raj told me when I went by to pick up a few additional things. "You'll be fine. Flying is safer than driving." He rattled off the statistics that always made me feel better.

"Thank you," I said. "For everything."

"It's not a big deal."

"Still, I appreciate it," I said, trying to soften my own formality.

"Look, if you need anything, just call me. Okay? I'm still here."

I'm still here. I repeat it until I fall asleep.

I wake to the sound of the captain's voice. Only an hour to New Delhi. I slide the window shade up. Dark dawn. Across the aisle Diwa is drinking coffee, smiling and laughing as he talks to the woman next to him. This, I realize, is the first time I've really seen him. He looks like Uncle and he looks like himself. Two people, but one.

Jyoti wakes, stretching inside the confines of her economy seat. "I'm so stiff. These seats are horrible." She looks up at the flight attendant who's just reached her with the beverage cart. "Coffee please, black." She pops a pill.

"What's that for?" I ask.

"Anxiety."

"I didn't know you had anxiety issues."

"I don't. A friend gave me these. She thought they'd help with my nerves."

"You know you shouldn't be taking someone else's medication."

"I've taken them before. I'll be fine."

"Still, you wouldn't believe how many people come into the hospital every day with drug complications."

Jyoti reaches over me as the attendant hands her the coffee. "Stop talking to me like you actually went to medical school."

I sigh and ask for a coffee as well.

"I'm sorry. You know I don't mean it. I'm just anxious, okay?" Jyoti reaches into her bag, pulls out a vial of lavender oil, and sniffs it. "Everyone says India is such an assault on the senses. I'm just worried—I don't want to freak out when we land."

"You won't freak out. Just don't make eye contact with anyone and keep walking. Don't stop."

She nods and douses her scarf in the oil.

Jyoti holds the scarf over her nose and mouth as we scurry through the crowds and out of the airport.

"Keep walking," I tell her again whenever she slows down. The locals seem to know she's vulnerable and call after her in broken English. She looks back at them, saying, "Sorry, sorry" over and over.

"Don't encourage them."

Diwa nudges her with the cart of suitcases. "Come on," he says, ignoring the faces and hands, the want and need.

"I can't believe this place," Jyoti says.

"Over there." I point to a man holding up a sign with our names on it.

"Is it safe?" Jyoti whispers as we approach.

"Yes, I told you, he's worked as a driver for Raj's family for years. Still, we should take shifts sleeping, just in case. It's a long drive."

"Shifts?" Jyoti begins to cry, muffling her mouth with the scarf. "I can't do this."

"You're doing just fine." I help her into the backseat and we drive for an hour before stopping for food and drink.

The tiny restaurant has cracked walls and reeks of frying oil and garbage, but the driver assures us that the food is good and, unlike the road-side carts, won't make us sick. Exhausted, we sit at a wooden table with mismatched chairs across from a group of elderly men playing cards. They are slight and worn through, faces weathered, toothless smiles, and yet they radiate some strange joy. I watch them as they slap cards down and laugh with their mouths wide open. The driver orders our food and then sits in the corner with the owner swapping stories and occasionally looking over at us to make sure we are okay. The air is heavy and what little circulation there is comes from the whirring of a single ceiling fan. Jyoti is leaning back in her chair, staring out through the dirty window at the beggars that sit by the road. Most are children. I don't ask her what she's thinking and when our food arrives, we pick at it in silence. After we've finished, the owner comes over and engages us in a dozen questioned pleasantries about where we are from and where we are going. Diwa answers them all without a hint of irritation.

"Twenty questions or what?" Jyoti says as we squeeze back into the car.

"He was only trying to be nice." I crack the window but the air that wafts in is ripe with sewage.

Jyoti covers her mouth until I slide the window shut. "Does everything smell like shit here?"

"Shh, he'll hear you," Diwa says as the driver gets in and starts the car.

Small fists bang on the window, children clamouring, hands gesturing to mouths.

"What do they want?" Jyoti asks the driver.

He blasts the horn and inches slowly out of his parking spot. "Food, ma'am. They want food."

Jyoti sits back and closes her eyes. Finally her pill takes effect and she's spared the last leg of the journey. Even I have to close my eyes and breathe deeply through the hairpin turns, the close calls with rickshaws and scooters.

It is nightfall when we arrive at Mother's family house.

The caretaker, a small, wiry man with pockmarked skin and bloodshot eyes, has been waiting; he welcomes us now into the courtyard. "Pleasant journey, ma'am?" he asks, his head see-sawing.

I nod and he quickly piles our suitcases onto a wooden cart. He starts to trundle it to the house, then turns back. "Do you remember me? We played soccer when you came here. Remember? You gave me the ball when you left."

"Of course," I say, though I don't recall this at all. "Diwa, Jyoti, this is . . ."

"Jasmeet," he supplies. He releases the cart for a moment and folds his hands in greeting.

"Your father worked here for many years, isn't that right?" I'm hoping I've got the details straight. "How is he? Is he well?" As I recite the polite questions Mother used to ask distant family and near strangers, I realize that what I always perceived as nosiness was just her way of showing interest.

"He is well, ma'am. Old now. He lives with me and my wife and children in the small house—your father's family house."

"How many children do you have?"

"Four boys," he says, bringing the cart up to the front door. "They help here on the farm and keep this house just as your parents instructed us."

"Do you still like it here?"

"Yes, very much. Most kind of your father to let us live in the house."

"It's you who do us the kindness of looking after everything."

He unlatches the door. "I have everything ready for you, all the furniture, floors, everything cleaned for you special." Jasmeet's eyes are following Diwa, who's wandered back into the courtyard and is staring at the sky. "My wife will come in the morning and bring you breakfast," he continues. "There are three bedrooms upstairs on the second floor and one on the third floor. Two washrooms. All water working, electricity working. Do you need me to show you anything?"

"No, that's fine." I look around the corner for Jyoti, who's already gone off exploring. "I'll see you in the morning."

"Not bad," Jyoti says from the living room. "All the modern conveniences. I didn't expect it to be so nice."

She's standing in front of the fan, venting her blouse. "But no AC. It's so hot!" Her voice reverberates in the fan blades. I sit across from her in the cane armchair, looking at the framed black-and-white photographs of our grandparents on the wall. They seem to stare back, eyes piercing through time.

Jyoti looks up. "Is that our grandmother?"

I nod.

"Wow, I've never seen a picture of her before. She looks so much like Mother." Jyoti picks up one of the smaller picture frames that grace the mantel. "And look at this one of Mother," she says.

"She's so young. What year do you think this was taken? Sharon looks like her, don't you think?" She replaces the photo and heads up the stairs. "I can't believe this is where Mother grew up," she calls out. "It's really nice—almost British India—you know, colonial. I was worried it would be more rural, mud walls and all that." Jyoti keeps on talking but I don't answer. I'm tired and relieved to have arrived. All of me craves sleep. I close my eyes and breathe in the scent of night-blooming jasmine.

"It's a small ceremony, but given the circumstances I suppose it's no cause for celebration," Dadi ji says as she twirls Amrita's hair into a bun. Amrita looks at her bridal self in the mirror. Her eyes are red from crying; Dadi ji has given up on lining them in kohl. "Even so, you mustn't cry. It's no one's fault. No one wanted this."

Amrita winces as Dadi ji pokes pins into her hair. "Father did."

"Wanting and needing are two different things, child. Your father, the boy's father, they are doing what needs doing. It's best for everyone."

"How do they know what is best?"

Dadi ji grabs Amrita by the chin, squishing her cheeks, her fat hands a muzzle. "You must stop this. You hear me, child? It's done. Right or wrong. Fair or unfair. You are marrying Manohor." She releases Amrita's face and reaches for the red-and-gold chunni. "Besides, what life would you have if you married Pyara? Have you thought about that?" She doesn't give Amrita a chance to answer. "No, of course you haven't. You've been so busy reading poems and watching Hindi movies that you think life is like that. It's not. Child, I assure you it's not." She stares at Amrita in the mirror. "Life is working, cooking, cleaning, eating, waking, sleeping, and dying. It does not involve feelings the way you young people think it does. It's a question of surviving. Making something out of whatever scraps you have. You should be grateful that your father has given you a chance to avoid such a hard fate. Taking care of a man who cannot take care of you is no life. His love will turn to resentment, and then what will you be left with? Nothing but your poems and books. How will you survive? Will Rumi help you then? Can these poems help you make a life?"

"Guru Nanak said that life was a journey toward finding God within oneself," Amrita says. "He didn't teach survival."

"Well, perhaps he was wrong. Maybe that's a fine purpose for men, but for women, our lives are simpler. We are born, we marry, we have children, and if we're lucky they have children, and then we die. At least your father gave you an education and is sending you away so that you can have a better life." Dadi ji places the embroidered chunni on Amrita's head, pulling it down over part of her face.

A veil or a shroud, Amrita can't decide. She looks down at her feet.

Amrita doesn't look up again, not even through the ceremony. No one sees her cry. Through her slow tears, she sees only feet. "One step at a time," she says under her breath as she walks the four Lavan, circling the scriptures and holding the pallu, the cloth that now joins her to this man she does not want.

It's only after the ceremony that she looks up, and only so that the photographer can take a picture. He counts down, says "Smile," but no one does.

That night, she sits on the bed still wearing her wedding clothes. She knows what comes next. The girls at boarding school read stories about it in the American magazines they'd smuggled into the dorm. One evening, Sonni, the prettiest girl at school, told them that in America, in one of her uncle's magazines, she'd seen pictures of people having sex. "Were they naked? What did it look like?" the girls asked. Sonni sat up in bed, the moonlight filtering through her nightie, outlining her perfect form. She gave a vivid description of what she saw, manoeuvring behind another girl to demonstrate the position. Her breasts bounced up and down. "That's awful," the girls squealed, hiding their scintillation.

Amrita shakes her head, jarring the memory. She's not excited, not nervous. Just frightened. When Manohor comes into the room he's already wearing his undershirt and pyjamas. Amrita squints, closing her eyes just enough so that she can imagine he's Pyara. The slight resemblance isn't enough, though, and makes her feel worse about what is to come.

"It's late," Manohor says, approaching the bed. He sits next to her and places his hand on her shoulder. After a moment she begins to unclasp her sari blouse. He watches her undo four hooks, his eyes trailing from hers down to the visible curve of her breast. He closes his eyes and reaches for her hand, pressing it to her chest. His breath is heavy. For a moment he says nothing, and she thinks she must have done something wrong. "You must be tired," he says and slowly gets up. He retrieves a mat from the wardrobe, rolls it out on the floor beside the bed, switches the lamp off, and lies down beneath a thin cotton sheet, his back to her.

She leans toward the edge of the bed, her wedding bracelets jingling in the dark, sounding each of her movements. "Husband," she whispers. Minutes go by. She tries again. "Husband."

"I cannot be your husband any more than you can be my wife."

Amrita rolls onto her back and stares at the ceiling, wondering whether Pyara is still awake in the small attic room above theirs. She hasn't seen him at all, and dared not inquire. Earlier she heard her mother-in-law climb the narrow stairs to take him his dinner and then later remark that he hadn't left his room all day, not even for the wedding. "Can you blame him?" her father-in-law said, scooping Pyara's uneaten daal and roti into his mouth. This house is much smaller than her own, its additions oddly placed, as if the house had been built one room at a time. The walls are so thin that sound seeps through and words carry, yet she hasn't heard his voice. Not a word.

Soon the house falls into a quiet sleep. But Amrita still lies awake, thinking how different it might have been, how different it was. She imagines Pyara, his hands and his lips. She makes him out of night and shadow, imagining him inside her, the sensation an ache and a longing. This feeling, so heavy, draws her to sleep, but when she wakes her pleasure dips, dissolving as quickly as the memory of that dream. She tries to hold on to it, but there is nothing left but night and shame.

In the morning Manohor is gone. Her mother-in-law, in the kitchen making paranthas, tells her that he's left for the city. "There is so much to arrange. Only three weeks until you leave. My cousin will meet him; he knows people who can help get the papers signed faster." She smiles, proud that her family can offer such help. She has mothered Pyara and Manohor since they were children, marrying their father only a year after he became a widower, a year after they settled in Punjab. She was only seventeen when they wed, but with her parents having died long ago, it was, for those times, a suitable marriage. "Then, when you're settled in the new country, you can sponsor us," she says, motioning to Amrita to help roll out the dough. Having never cooked before, Amrita struggles. "You will learn," her mother-in-law says with a big laugh, taking the rolling pin from her to demonstrate. "No servants here to do the work for you, heh? We will see how much your degree helps you now." She laughs again. Amrita soon realizes that she laughs after everything she says, a shrill and wicked postscript. "I already have family abroad. My sister and her husband live there, you know, but with Manohor there too, it will be easier to get over now."

Amrita nods. "What about the farm?"

Her mother-in-law looks at her sideways. "Many years to think about that. Manohor's father will soon be too old to care for it, and with no sons here—no able-bodied sons—it will make sense for us to sell and leave this place."

"And what of Pyara? What will become of him?"

Her mother-in-law shrugs. "He will marry. We will find a girl who can take care of him. He is still a good match for someone with no options."

Amrita focuses on trying to roll out the dough in a perfect circle.

"Here, why don't you take this to Pyara," her mother-in-law says minutes later, handing her a breakfast tray with hot tea and her crooked parantha. "Since you're so concerned about him." She laughs once more.

Amrita climbs the two flights of stairs to the small room. She balances the tray and knocks twice. No answer. She sets down the tray, presses her ear against the door, and whispers urgently: "Pyara, it's Amrita. Please open the door." No answer. "Your mother has sent me to give you your breakfast."

"Leave it at the door and go," he yells.

"Open the door and I can help you." She's hoping for just a look at his face.

"I said leave it."

"As you wish." She makes her way back to the kitchen, where her mother-in-law is placing paranthas in a tiffin.

"Take these to Manohor's father," she instructs, handing her the tin containers. "He's working in the fields farthest from the house. Hurry so they don't get cold."

Amrita nods, but just as she's about to leave she hears the clattering of dishes above her. She rushes up the stairs, leaving her mother-in-law's voice and laughter behind. "That's right, girl, run and see what you find there."

Pyara's door is open. He's sitting on the floor, the contents of his taal spilled around him. Amrita kneels and picks up the steel dishes, returning them to the tray. She doesn't look at him, not at first.

"Let me help."

Pyara stares straight ahead through the open balcony door, across the swaying fields. She gets up and places his tray on the table. His room is sparsely furnished—a wardrobe, a cot, a wobbly table, a simple chair. In the corner stands the wooden cane she'd made especially for him when she still thought there was a chance they would marry. He struggles to hoist himself up on the edge of his cot. One pyjama leg is twisted and pinned at the stump. He manoeuvres his limbs and shifts his weight, trying to sit comfortably, beads of sweat forming on his brow. When Amrita approaches him he holds her back with a look. "Your help does me no good," he says. Then he unravels the pyjama leg and shows her the bandaged twist and knot of flesh, not fully healed.

She doesn't flinch. "Does it hurt?"

"Sometimes I can feel pain in my leg even though the leg is gone. The doctor calls it phantom pains."

"How is that possible?"

"The same way you feel things that aren't there," he says, staring through her. "The way you feel things here." He presses his fist to his chest, pounding it slowly, rhythmically, as if trying to make his own heart beat. "It's phantom pain. We feel what doesn't exist."

"It exists."

"No. It's only a trick of the mind—just a memory. The mind cannot distinguish between what is and what is imagined."

"And did we imagine it?"

"Let's say we did. For everyone's sake." He ties up his pyjama again, covering his lame leg. "The pain will get better in time."

"Or maybe that's just another trick of the mind. Nothing gets better. You just get used to it."

"Perhaps."

Her mother-in-law shouts up the stairs: "Amrita, the food is getting cold. Hurry, you must deliver it on time."

"Coming," she calls, then picks up Pyara's tray of toppled dishes and spilled tea. "I'll ask her to bring you another one."

"Shut the door on your way out."

She begins to leave.

"And, Amrita."

"Yes?" Hopeful, she turns toward him.

He gazes at her for a moment and then looks away as if he's ashamed. "Don't come again."

She lowers her head, unsure whether the shame is his or hers alone, and then rushes down the stairs to hand the tray to her mother-in-law.

"What a mess he's made. I suppose he'll want more?"

"He's not hungry," Amrita says simply. She picks up her father-in-law's steel lunch containers. As she crosses the field, she doesn't look back.

The emergency room is full of the usual two a.m. cross-section: mothers and their fevered children, last-call bruisers, runaway junkies, the elderly. Raj is getting coffee from the vending machine, Diwa is sitting with Mother, and I'm at reception answering questions, filling in forms.

"Take a seat," the admitting nurse says. She doesn't look up from her keyboard, the glare of the computer screen bouncing off her glasses.

"How long?" I strain across the counter to see what she's typing. Part of me wants to leap over the desk and key in the information myself.

"At least an hour," she says. "Smith. Robert Smith," she calls. As a man who smells of urine and vomit approaches the desk I walk away, giving him a wide berth.

I sit across from Mother. "How long?" she asks.

"An hour, but it could be sooner." I explain the inner workings of emergency room triage.

"So they see the sickest person first." She shakes her head. "I told you we shouldn't have come."

"If you'd agreed to come in the ambulance with the paramedics, we wouldn't be waiting at all," I point out.

"No need for an ambulance when you can drive me. Ambulances are for sick people. I fell down. That's all."

I wonder why she's speaking in such short sentences. A possible concussion, I think. An easy symptom to miss in a slammed ER. Wanting to jot it down, I walk back to the counter and ask to borrow a pen and paper. The admitting nurse glares at me. I smile as I reach over the counter, snatch a pen, and write "Concussion?" on the back of my hand. I return the pen before sitting down again.

"Best to get these things checked," Diwa says, attempting to reassure Mother.

"I suppose. But at least we could have gone to Simran's hospital. That way I could see where she works. All these years I've never been there. Can you believe it?"

"I'm sure she'll take you for a visit soon."

She nods, always less likely to argue with him. He's been home for six months and she's never been happier. It wasn't the tearful reunion I expected, but nor was there any trace of anger or bitterness. Later, I asked Mother if they'd talked about it.

"It?" she said. "What do you mean, it?"

"The past. Everything that happened."

"Nothing happened. The past is past is past."

When I challenged her on it, she reminded me that she was dying. "I'm not spending what little time I have left talking about things I can't change. It's time to move on."

Raj hands me a cup of coffee. "It's bad. Just warning you."

"Anything is good this early in the morning."

Raj sits back in his chair and closes his eyes. I flip through the dated current-event magazines.

Mother's eyes are closed. "Wake up," I say, shaking her shoulder. She opens one eye. "I wasn't asleep."

I explain that if she's had a concussion, she needs to stay awake. "Amrita Sandhu?"

A nurse in heart-patterned scrubs stands by the desk with a chart. She calls Mother's name again, and the way she says it—the loud, fat syllables—makes her sound agitated. I get up quickly, waving my hand so that she doesn't call the next name on her chart. We all step forward and follow her into another holding area, then finally, after another thirty minutes, to a bed where Mother is handed a hospital gown.

"She can change in there." The nurse points to a draped cubicle.

Diwa and Raj move to help Mother out of the hospital wheelchair. "One, two, lift," I say as they each support her under an arm. I grab a nearby walker and we shuffle to the change room. "Okay, I've got it from here," I tell them.

Mother sits down on the little bench. I lift each of her arms, pull off her shirt, and help her into the gown. "All this for nothing," she says. "You'll see, they will tell me I'm fine. They will say be more careful."

"Mother, please." I realize that I'm sweating from the exertion. "Put your arms around my neck." When she reluctantly complies, I hoist her up just enough so that I can slide her pants down around her hips.

"I'm like a sack of potatoes now," she says as I sit her back down. "Something to move from here to there."

"Don't be ridiculous." I pull her trousers past her knees, only then realizing that I've forgotten her shoes. I kneel down to undo her laces and take each shoe off, working quickly, mechanically, the way I would at the hospital when turning patients in their bed, always on the count of three and never looking them in the eye. I shimmy her pants over her ankles and pull them off, losing my own balance momentarily. Then I steady myself and fold her clothes, placing them in the plastic bag they've provided. Finally I pull the curtain back and grab the walker again.

"Okay, up one more time," I say. "Ready?"

She nods like a person who has no choice.

Once more I put her arms around my neck and help her up. She reaches for the walker with one hand and then the other. "Got it?" I ask.

"Of course." She shuffles to the hospital bed as I steady her walker with one hand. When I look to see if I've forgotten anything I catch our reflection in the change-room mirror: the open back of Mother's hospital gown, her knotty spine and alabaster skin, her white knee-high socks, her beige Sears underwear so big now that they hang off her behind. I reach around with my free hand and pull the gown closed.

The four of us wait for another hour, listening to the sounds of bed curtains opening and closing, machines beeping, gurney wheels squeaking, nurses' soft shoes and loud laughter. The endless talk and woe of pain. "Where does it hurt?"

I watch the futility of it all playing out around me. The nurses and doctors, the attendants and technicians—all well-meaning, all wanting to help, all just like me. But over time, the "wanting to help" leaves a residue. Too few wins stacked against mounting losses. I can still remember my first patient who died: Patricia, with the loud voice and red hair. One day she was there at the end of my shift, and the next her bed had been stripped and was being readied for a new patient. No goodbyes.

Finally the curtain is pulled back and Dr. Williams introduces himself. Unlike the others, he makes eye contact and listens intently as Mother tries to tell him how she fell. "Just lost my balance," she explains in her broken English. "Bumped my head."

"That's quite a bruise," he says, looking at the scrape on her forehead.

"She fell forward, over her walker," Diwa puts in.

I hadn't realized that's how she fell. I hadn't asked. By the time I had arrived, the ambulance was outside and the front door to the house was wide open. The paramedics had Mother sitting up and were checking her vitals.

"It's a good thing you were there," Dr. Williams says to Diwa. "You got lucky. It could have been much worse." He flashes a light in each of her eyes and then holds up two fingers. "How many?"

"Two."

"Good." He moves on to other questions. There is something about his attentiveness that reminds me of Charles, and for a minute I'm lost in the guilt of that time and don't hear Raj call my name.

"What?" I can feel my face flush.

"Your mother's neurologist is Dr. Clarkson, right? So the doctor can send the notes over."

"Yes, that's right," I stammer. Then I glance down at the reminder scribbled on my hand. "What about a concussion? Could she have had one?"

"It's always a possibility, but she seems fine. Falls are common given your mother's condition." Dr. Williams scribbles on the chart. "But still, we'll send the notes over so that your doctor has a record of it."

"Thank you," we say in a staggered unison.

"Well, that's that then," I say after he's left. I begin the complicated choreography involved in getting her dressed again.

"See, I'm fine," Mother says later as Diwa wheels her out of the hospital. "Just a bruise."

Raj reaches for my arm and links it in his, slowing me down. He lowers his voice. "She's right, you know. She *is* fine."

"Still, it was good to get it checked out." I zip up my jacket against the morning cold.

"Sim, this is all part of the disease," he whispers. "You know there's nothing that can be done for her. She's going to keep falling."

I stop and turn to him. "What? So you're suggesting that if she falls, we do nothing?"

"No, that's not what I said." He waits until Diwa and Mother are out of earshot. "I'm saying that if she falls and gets a bruise or a scrape, we pick her up and allow her to keep living on her own terms for as long as she can."

"I just wanted to make sure she was all right."

"But she's not." He reaches for my hand. "And nothing they can say will make her all right and nothing they say will make you all right with the fact that she's dying. Don't make her come here and face that every time she falls."

"I don't want to talk about this now." I pull away from him and walk to the car in silence.

It's easy to lose myself here. The sky goes on forever, the sunsets stretch like a veil across the horizon between all that was and all that is, the fields at night a black sea swaying beneath an ancient map of stars. This place has quieted my thoughts, as if someone has laid softness inside me and everything is a whisper of solitude. The days are long, but when night comes, it descends quickly and my silence becomes sleep. A forgotten rhythm now remembered. Everything else falls away. This morning a mist hovered over the fields, creeping through the tall grass, apparitions dissolving as the sun cast its glow.

"Did you see the sunrise?" I ask at breakfast.

Jyoti nods, sipping her tea. "It's hard to sleep here, isn't it?"

"Awake with the sun, asleep with the moon." I turn to Diwa. "That's what Mother used to say when she woke us up to do weekend chores, remember?"

"I don't remember that," Jyoti says before Diwa can respond.

"She hated housework," I continue. "She used to make a game out of it for us. Whoever did the most chores would get to choose what we watched on TV that night."

"You always won," Diwa says. "But you let me watch my shows anyway."

"*Happy Days*—can't go wrong with the Fonz." Diwa and I smile at each other as we raise Fonzie's signature thumbs-up and imitate his signature *Ehhhh*.

Jyoti sighs. "I missed out—only watched it in reruns."

Diwa laughs. "You should be glad. Once he jumped the shark it went downhill."

After breakfast we take a walk, single file, through the fields toward the banyan tree. The sun is climbing, and with each step I can feel a thread of perspiration weaving down my neck and trickling down my back. Yet my breathing is steady and full, and for the first time since we arrived I feel as though I'm fully inhabiting my body. Everything is alive. I squint my eyes and look up at the massive tree towering above its lush surroundings. We make our way through its gnarled roots and branches, grasping arthritic grey limbs as we duck under and over. I gaze up at the green canopy where light filters through the leaves and birds nest and call.

None of us says anything.

We each find our own place to sit. Jyoti prays, Diwa writes poetry, and I listen. If I close my eyes, I can see it all unfold before me. This is the place where they fell in love. "Under a tree that keeps dividing and growing and becoming." That's how Mother described it. Her talk was mostly nonsensical at the end, and when I told her I didn't understand, she said, "Be patient." Then she looked up, her eyes searching, reimagining. "We read poetry. He knew them by heart—Tagore, Rumi, Gibran, all the greats. He wanted to be a professor. But back then you did as your family said. His father said, 'Be an engineer,' and so he became an engineer . . . *To have loved you in numberless forms, numberless times . . . In life after life . . . You become an image of what is remembered forever.* Tell me, how could I not have fallen in love . . . It was our fault, we killed him."

"I don't understand," I said again, leaning in, resting my head on the bed rails.

"Of course you don't."

"Whatever it was, I'm sure it wasn't your fault."

"Then whose, if not ours? Sometimes I think we all died that day. Sometimes I think everything that was good and possible died that very night."

"That's not true."

"You're right. Life finds a way, doesn't it?"

"I don't know what you mean."

"You do. You always did. We aren't who we seem to be."

"If that's true, then who are we?"

She shrugged. "A question best left for the poets."

"What about Diwa's poems? What were they about?" I was trying to piece it all together.

She sighed, falling into the mystery of herself. Her stories went on, unravelling in a coil, stretching and collapsing until she could no longer speak. Not long after that she was placed in hospice, and the waiting began. "Talk to her," the nurses said. "She still understands you." But when I did, all I saw was her pained expression, her longing for the end, her desperation. Then I didn't know what to say. I would talk about the weather—the haze and fog, say, that had lingered over the city for twenty straight days, the fine mist and steady dew in the air, the uneasy feeling of not being able to see more than five feet in front of you. I was always glad when Diwa arrived; he read her poetry. When Jyoti came for the occasional visit, she would turn on Mother's favourite soap opera. I'd spend the rest of the day sitting in the lounge, drinking cups of tea out of mismatched china. "It's not an easy thing to know what to do," the nurse said once when she saw me take a swig from a flask between sips of tea. "Dying doesn't come naturally to any of us."

"I'm sorry. I know how this must look."

"What it looks like is that you're trying to cope."

"Trying to, yes."

"There is no right way. You just have to do whatever it takes to get through. No judgments."

I took another sip before going back to the hospital room. Diwa was reading his new poem, inspired by Gibran.

> *Toward that great end*
> *the place of our longing, where*
> *time is no measure.*

> *Toward that great end*
> *Wander and return*
> *Whence it came.*

Whence it came. Now, as I look around at the branches becoming root and root becoming limb, I realize that it's a life of returns. "She left only to come back." That's what Jasmeet said when he learned we'd crossed the ocean carrying Mother's ashes. "And now she will follow her ancestors home." He walked with us one morning at dawn, showing us the river where our grandfather's ashes were scattered, where Pyara's ashes were scattered. "What about our grandmother's ashes?" Jyoti asked.

"Your father's mother—she died in childbirth. Her ashes were scattered in Pakistan—in India, before Partition. Your mother's mother, your nani, was left behind. There was no time for proper cremation."

Jyoti looked confused. "I don't understand."

"I should not say. It's not my place."

"Please."

He folded his hands, asking forgiveness even before he began. "During Partition, your grandmother was kidnapped in a raid. Some of the women jumped into the well, killed themselves so they wouldn't be captured, but your grandmother was heavy with child and could not run. They cut her open, pulled the baby boy right out of her, and left him lying in a pile of her innards."

Jyoti covered her mouth, looking as if she was going to be sick. After a moment she turned to me. "Did you know about this?"

"No, not all of it."

She glared.

"I knew only that she was killed during Partition. Even Mother didn't talk about it."

"Why would she?" Diwa said. "It's all so horrific."

Jasmeet nodded. "No one speaks of it. We all want to forget. I should not have repeated it."

He walked upriver, and we followed him all the way back to the farm, the sun rising unceremoniously above us, silver light against low clouds. We decided we would scatter the ashes the following day. But that day came and went, and still her ashes remain sealed in the box.

Today, we decide we'll do it tomorrow. "Time is running out," I say. "We leave in less than a week."

"I didn't think it would be so hard," Jyoti says. "It's like we're leaving her behind. Like it's really over."

THEN

It's the year when everything dies on the vine. Snow blankets early. The snapping of twigs, still green on the inside, echoes like the cracking of bone. The sound of a single moment and life swallowed whole. I look out at the few leaves still clinging to branches, trembling in the wind.

Mother taps the window, counting out the leaves—thousands were blown down by the windstorm, thousands are rotting beneath the perfect snow—and now she's numbering each one with a smudge on the glass. Twenty-five left. She says it over and over again. Diwa's sitting at the kitchen table reading the newspaper. He holds the paper close to his face as if he's concentrating, just the way I taught him when he was a child. "Sound it out," I'd say with only the slightest irritation, except then he didn't know what that was. He hadn't learned that there was a word for what people felt around him. "Clear and cold," he reads out now. "Low minus four, a high of six." He glances up at me. "It will be a nice afternoon after all."

I look at him, searching. I look at him the way a woman looks at a man who's lost in the world, except he's not lost, it's me who's lost. He's rooted in this life. Before returning to us, the hotel rooming house was home. He had his routines. He'd made his own life out of the scraps he was given. And still he agreed to quit his job at the library, to come home. For me and for Mother. He puts the paper down and picks up his cane.

He found it packed in the attic when he returned to the house. We'd left it there as children. "This is why Father sent me away," he told me. "It wasn't because of my handicap, or my poems, it was this cane."

"Do you remember anything else?"

"No, not much. Only that I hit him with it. I also remember the day they left me there at Bibi Jeet's. I chased that car for half a mile before I realized they weren't going to stop."

"Have you asked Mother about it?"

He paused. I waited tentatively, hoping he'd found some understanding of the events of his life.

"No. She's so weak now."

I nodded.

"Do *you* remember?" he asked.

"No more than you." I was half lying. I didn't want to be the one to put the pieces of his life together, to burden this life with the last. What good could come of it, other than the realization that we're powerless against our own mystery? "I remember you hitting him, and Mother asking me to take care of you. We slept in my bed. You cried yourself to sleep."

I didn't give him the details of how that night began. I didn't tell him that when Father came home Mother ushered us out from under the kitchen table where we were playing cars. "Quick," she said. "Go play in the attic. Your father is in a mood." This usually meant he was drunk and not to be bothered. From the attic, where we were playing Charlie Chaplin with Diwa's cane, we could hear him yelling that his dinner was cold. As his voice grew louder Diwa got curious. He began to creep down the steps. "Come back," I whispered, following him. "You're going to get us in trouble." Diwa didn't listen. He was standing at the end of the hallway, peering around the corner into the kitchen, watching Mother and Father argue.

"What? You are too smart to make a simple meal? Did they forget to teach you that in college?" Father's face was close to hers.

"If you don't like my cooking, make it yourself!"

Father knocked his dishes off the counter and grabbed her by the hair. "Now clean it up!" he yelled. "Can you do that? Or is that beneath you?"

"Let her go!" Diwa rushed into the room, charging at Father with his cane.

Surprised, Father fell back. Diwa hit him on the head with the cane repeatedly. Finally, Father grabbed it from him.

"Where did you get this?" he asked, a look of horror on his face.

"It's mine. Everything you have is mine! You stole everything. It's mine!"

Mother was wild with panic, telling Diwa to stop yelling. I cowered in the doorway, curious and frightened.

"Stop!" Father yelled, and then he struck Diwa down.

"Manohor hit me," Diwa cried, flying into Mother's arms. Mother unlatched him from her, one arm at a time, telling him to calm himself. Then she called out to me to take him upstairs.

The next day Diwa was sent away.

———

Diwa holds the cane in his right hand. He pulls himself up from the table, lurches forward, and steadies himself. Then, pulling his bad leg behind him—in an almost distinguished gait compared to his childhood limp—he heads across the kitchen. What made him lame as an awkward child makes him more interesting as a man. He stands at the window with Mother, staring out at the tree, at the open blue sky.

I glance at him, admiring again what a handsome man he's become. He has a smooth olive complexion and longish hair tucked behind his ears—a style that men don't wear anymore. Everything about him is from another time.

"What shall we do today, Mother? Shall we go for a walk?" he asks.

When Mother nods, Diwa wheels her chair toward me. I help her put on her coat and boots and position the chair. "Ready?" I ask.

"I'd like to walk today," she says triumphantly.

"Mother, please, you don't want to waste your energy."

"It's mine to waste, isn't it?"

"Yes, but you remember what the doctor said. You've already fallen three times this week. You have to be careful."

"I'll walk while I still can. Now, shall we go or are you staying here?"

"Okay. Have it your way." I throw my coat on.

Outside the air is crisp, our breath visible. The shoveled sidewalk is dusted in frost, twinkling like shards of crystal. Mother is using Diwa's cane. She leans on him, linking her arm in his. From behind, I can't make out who is holding up whom.

"It's much colder there," Manohor explains as relatives pore over the contents of the suitcases and trunks. Their grubby hands finger Amrita's winter coat and hand-knitted sweaters.

"And the tava and pot." Her mother-in-law holds them up. "They cannot buy these in Canada—so few Indians," she explains to the small horde of aunts, cousins, and second cousins. Eyes wide, they nod knowingly.

"You must be excited," a cousin says to Amrita.

Her mother-in-law answers for her. "Of course she's excited. Who wouldn't be? In Canada everyone is rich and it snows."

"Snow? Like in Shimla?" another cousin asks.

"I've been to Shimla," a third cousin chimes in. "It's not like the Hindi movies where everyone dances on the mountains with no jackets. It's too cold for that."

"How do you know? Have you tried it?" an auntie asks.

Amrita leaves the room as they burst out laughing. She boils water for tea, glad to be put into service by her mother-in-law, who is busy enjoying her celebrity. By now most of the village has come to the house. "They come because they want a sponsorship for their children and their children's children," Dadi ji said during yesterday's visit, after having endured an hour of Mother-in-law's boasting.

"Perhaps, but isn't that why your granddaughter married our son?" Mother-in-law said.

Dadi ji shook her head in the way you would expect of an ancient. "My son allowed the marriage out of respect to your family. It was an honourable arrangement. Or have you forgotten?" She motioned upward, calling attention to Pyara's movements above. "Had it not been for any of that, none of this would have happened. Amrita would have settled into a different situation."

Mother-in-law smiled and laughed through her teeth. "Of course, no need to get upset. Amrita, get your dadi ji more tea," she said, relegating her to the small hovel of a room that had become a sanctuary from the onlookers and money grabbers.

"Everyone wants something," Manohor says now as he walks into the kitchen with a little notepad. He holds it up. "It's a list of names and things to bring back when or if we return to India for a visit."

"We haven't even left and already they await our return," Amrita says.

He smiles but quickly turns away, returning to their guests. All week he's avoided her company. And yet a familiarity has been growing. "We are married whether we like it or not," he said after hearing that his stepmother chastised Amrita for not consummating the marriage. "But it is too soon for us to act like it."

Each night he sleeps on the floor and each morning he's gone before Amrita wakes. He's industrious, attempting to do the work of two brothers. Already he's hired several village boys to help on the farm; he'll send money back to pay for their keep. And every evening he sits with Pyara, each reading silently. They talk very little. But every time Manohor leaves, Pyara says the same thing: "It's not your fault, brother."

Amrita repeats this phrase in her head whenever she looks at him. "It's not your fault." She repeats it as she stands in front of the mirror brushing her hair. "It's not your fault." But no matter how many times she says it, she doesn't believe it.

"Will we be cursed?" she asked her dadi ji on the morning of the wedding.

"No, child. No curse but the one you swear on yourself." Dadi ji held up Amrita's chin in the way she always did when she was serious. "Understand me?"

Even now, every time she sees Pyara she swears off happiness the way holy men swear off temptation. She reminds herself of this vow when she serves the tea to the guests, when they congratulate her on leaving for Canada, and when she wakes up the next morning to the first glow of dawn.

The walls are washed in light, so bright that at first she can't open her eyes. She blinks rapidly, adjusting to the morning, listening to the house sparrows. Upstairs, Pyara is awake. She hears the balcony door open and imagines him watching the sunrise. She hears the thump of his cane, something scraping against the floor, and then silence. She sits up and looks at Manohor sleeping on the floor next to her.

Just as she's about to lie back down, a loud clatter comes from above. Manohor bolts awake and rushes upstairs. "Brother, are

you all right?" he asks through the closed door. Amrita is standing at the bottom of the stairs now. He looks back at her before
knocking on the door again. "Brother." He presses his ear against
the door, and when he hears nothing he twists the handle. It
doesn't open. "Brother," he says, more urgently now. He pushes
his weight against the door again and again until finally it opens
and he staggers into the room. "No!"

Amrita runs up the stairs. Her father-in-law and mother-in-
law call out from below: "What's happening?" She doesn't answer.

There are no words.

Pyara is hanging from the ceiling fan, a rope wrapped tight
around his throat, his foot twitching as he spins. Manohor rights
the overturned chair and then steps up on it. He wraps his arms
around Pyara's hips, hoisting his brother's body, trying to allevi-
ate the strain and suffocation. Amrita is paralyzed. Her mother-
in-law is screaming. Manohor yells to his father to bring a knife.

His father cuts the rope. Pyara topples onto his brother. They
collapse onto the floor in a broken heap.

"Don't leave us, brother," Manohor cries, scrambling to his knees.

Pyara is motionless, heavy with death. Still Manohor tries to
revive him, passing his own breath into his mouth.

"Please, brother."

No response.

He shakes him.

No response.

Another breath.

No response.

No sound except for their own ragged breath and open-mouthed
sobs. Manohor is crying too now, tears streaming down his face.
He is gasping for air, begging for mercy. None comes.

———

The house falls into mourning. The family dresses in white. Amrita takes off her wedding bracelets and throws them in the river.

Manohor lights the funeral pyre. Heat rises. Black smoke billows.
Amrita watches over Pyara as his body is consumed by fire.
She does not wail. She does not weep.
She watches as his ashes are taken to the river.
She watches him sink, and then flow.
How quickly he moves away from her.
All the villagers talk. It's her fault. It's Manohor's fault. It's Pyara's fault.
God is blameless.

Wе wake up in the pre-dawn. The only words spoken are "It's time to go." Diwa leads us through the cool darkness of the fields toward the river, weaving through the rows that sway like the sea. We are dressed in white cotton, a stark single file against the blue shadows of morning. I carry the ashes. Jyoti carries a copper bowl and marigold garlands. Diwa carries a lantern. We don't know how to do this but we are beholden to the silence of this place. We wait for first light, a gilded horizon. The birds sound their calls. The river shimmers as though lit from below, from fallen stars and ancient light.

I kneel in the grass and open the box, tentatively breaking the plastic seal. As I pour the contents into the copper bowl, ash and soot rise in small puffs of smoke. I inhale and stand up, offering the bowl to Diwa. He takes his sandals off and walks into the water. We follow a few steps behind. The river is cold but alive, swarming around us. We walk past the tall grass, beyond the rocky riverbed, until we are knee deep, our feet pressing into the mud below.

Taking turns, we scoop the ashes out of the bowl and cup them in our open palms. What the wind does not take we let slip from our fingers into the water, to drift and flow. My hands are covered in chalky dust. I turn them over, examining what remains. Jyoti scatters the marigolds. Diwa sets the tea light from the lantern into the water. We stand, grey-handed, watching it all float away.

Jyoti and Diwa wash the remains from their hands, holding them under the water. When they pull them out they are pink and clean, newborn. I don't wash my hands right away. I let ash cake into my palms, charting lines.

We walk back, away from the eastern sun, our heads down, eyes cast at dirt.

The downpour begins just as we get to the house. First, claps of thunder. Then rain, falling in heavy sheets like streams of silverfish. We rush inside and stay there for the day. The power is intermittent. Jasmeet's wife brings us food and tea. Day turns to night. We sit in the living room and light candles. We play cards and read books from the stacks that line Grandfather's study.

"It's quite a collection," I say, running my fingers across a row, their spines perfectly aligned. "It looks like he organized it by category: economics, engineering, and, over here, history and literature." I pull a book from the lower shelf and blow the dust from its jacket. "*Philosophy of Religion.* It's odd—Mother always made him out to be such a practical man, someone who didn't have time for anything like this. And yet all these books—and in English too. He must have gone to some lengths to get them." I flip through the pages. "Chapter Two: The Case for God." I read silently for a moment and then snap the book shut. "Do you believe in God?"

Diwa is tending the fire. He's just added a new log and the sparks fly up. "Who are you asking?" He pokes the log into place.

"Either of you."

Jyoti looks up from her reading. "You know I do."

"But why?" I lean in closer so that I can see her face in the dim light. She is gold and shadows.

"I don't know. I just do."

I replace the book on its shelf and sit next to her, waiting for a real answer.

"It was never a conscious choice. Not like *you* think it was . . . For me, it was a way to be connected. Sometimes I think that maybe I turned to the church because I wanted to belong to something. I guess, in a way, growing up I felt I was always on the outside." She says this slowly, looking at both of us. "But in the church you feel like you're on the inside. That you really matter."

"You do matter," I say.

"I know that now." She reaches for my hand. "And do you?"

"Matter?"

"I mean, do you believe in God?"

"I believe in something." I lean back on the sofa, looking at our shadows on the wall. "But no, not God. Not in the way people think of God. Not in absolutes." I pause. "Sometimes I wish I did believe. It would make life so much easier."

"Faith isn't easy," Jyoti says. "It's a struggle to keep believing, to have hope."

"I didn't mean to offend." I'm worried that I've upset her, that I've broken this delicate balance of understanding between us.

"I know that. But don't you see? Life gives you so many reasons to not believe in anything, so many reasons to give in. I think it's the surrendering to that helplessness that would be easy."

"Not knowing or believing in God isn't helplessness." I pull my hand away from hers.

"No, you're right, it's not. It's loneliness." Her eyes are downturned.

Shame sits in my stomach like balled-up energy, all worry and anxiety. "Is that how you see me—as lonely?" I swallow hard.

"Aren't you?" she presses.

"Sometimes. Sure. But just because I'm alone doesn't mean I'm lonely. For the first time in my life I'm taking time to figure out what I want."

"And have you figured it out?"

"No, but I'm trying. I think I've always been scared of being alone, and I don't want to be frightened. I want to know what it's like to be independent."

"Independence is a myth," Diwa says suddenly. He gets up from the fireside, his shadow falling over Jyoti and me as he sits across from us. "People mistake independence for freedom. It's not the same."

I study him closely. "Tell us, then. What do you believe, Diwa?"

"I believe what the poets tell us. They speak of love and divinity and truth. That's real freedom."

"That sounds like God to me," Jyoti says, raising her arms in the air as if she were an evangelical.

"What about the afterlife?" I ask.

No one speaks. We are all quiet. Thinking of Mother.

The candlelight flickers. Diwa clears his throat. "After I ran away I lived on the streets, sleeping on benches or under overpasses for years. And even though charities and churches handed out blankets, I never made much of God or man. But eventually I got lucky and moved to a rooming house on the lower east side.

There was this guy who lived there—he was a scientist, or so he claimed. I don't know what his real name was—none of us there went by our real names. We called him Einstein. Anyway, he didn't say much, mumbling mostly about energy theories. And when he was scratching out formulas on a chalkboard tablet in his lap, he'd whisper, *Energy can neither be created nor destroyed but transforms from one form to another.* He said it over and over again. He was trying to find the mathematical equation for creation."

"He was trying to solve our origins?" Jyoti leans forward, fighting against the light and shadows that shroud us all.

"Strange, right? But it got me thinking about death—that maybe we're just energy, and that when we die our energy finds a new form."

"Like reincarnation," I say, hoping to spark his memory of something.

"Maybe. It seems plausible. We've all had that feeling of having been somewhere before. Even here, something about this place seems so familiar."

"I don't know—reincarnation seems far-fetched," Jyoti says.

"As far-fetched as an old bearded man in the sky," I add, grinning.

Jyoti smiles, and it feels good to see her relax into opposing ideas. "Diwa, did Einstein ever finish his equation?"

"Don't know. He burned the building down during one of his experiments and ended up in the psych ward. Turns out he wasn't even a scientist."

We break into laughter.

"But no one was who they said they were anyway. Everyone was running away from something, half crazy, half scared, sometimes both."

"That must have been hard." Jyoti gets up and pours herself a cup of tea from the pot left on the table. "Living on your own at such a young age. I can't imagine." She takes a sip. "Want some?" Diwa nods and she hands him a cup. I shake my head and move closer to the fire, poking the logs until sparks become flame. "What was it like?" Jyoti asks.

"Being on my own? I never really thought about it. I knew if I did, it would make me crazy."

"I've never heard you talk about your life much."

"No point in dwelling in the past. Life makes you do things you're not proud of."

"I'm sorry."

"Sorry for what? It's not your fault. You were just a kid."

"I could have made an effort when you came back, but I was jealous. Mother loved you and she didn't even notice me."

"Jyoti, that's not true," I say, looking over at her. "She loved us all."

"Yes, she loved us all but it was Diwa she loved the most."

We fall silent. It's the truth.

"And what did that get me? You said it yourself: I lived alone most of my life. And maybe, in a way, so did you, and even you, Simran. We've all lived alone."

Our silence collects, has its own shadow.

Jyoti speaks first. "And what is God other than an answer or a reason in the dark?"

Mother is disappearing deep inside her breath. Hidden now inside a cage of bones, bird-breasted, slip-limbed. Her face is sinking, all hollows and edges, the visible pulse on her temple flickering, a memory and the route it travels. I wonder what she sees now that her eyes are fixed at closed. Is she imagining, dreaming, listening? Can she hear me tell her that I love her, I'm sorry, I love her, I'm sorry? It's all that matters. A reconciliation so that she can die and stop this drift. That's what I imagine it as—floating, or bobbing in the water, voices dunking, drifting like an old melody with forgotten words.

Exhale. Her breath rattles.

The nurses come in and pull back the curtains, reposition her, manoeuvre limbs, stack pillows, fold legs and arms, check her breathing. She is her body and they marvel at how it still holds her. They speak to her as if she'll answer and I feel ashamed for always filling in the gaps, for always answering for her. For talking and telling and speaking and wanting. Today the nurse is Ivy. She is as vibrant as her name suggests. Her kind manner and voice are tendrils I want to hold on to. Mother never met her, not really, but still Ivy speaks with familiarity and affection, adding "dears" and "sweethearts" to the end of phrases. They catch on my heart the way a stray thread pulls on an old sweater. "I'm just going to turn you, dear." "I'm just going to give you a quick wash and freshen you up, sweetheart." Ivy applies lotions and creams to keep Mother's skin soft, to keep it from cracking the way the soles of her feet have cracked, like tough earth and pounded desert. She hangs the new medication on the pole and I watch the slow intravenous drip. The intricate feed of sedation through tube, through skin and vein and blood. I note the bruised IV sites on her arms—a map, charting illness.

These are the end stages.

The last days of the last weeks of the last months of the last years.

Soon it will be over, but I don't know what that even means. Ivy counts Mother's breath, times it on her delicate gold wristwatch. I write it down in my book, I keep a detailed log of everything, holding on to her with clinical controls. Diwa writes them on his slips of paper. He makes them into poems, into something better than seconds and minutes, but all I do is count down daylights, twilights, go to the light, go to the light.

Her breath is ragged.

I want to lift her, carry her, offer her up to the spirits of my ancestors. I call their names. I learn their prayers. "Satnam Vaheguru." I say it over and over again. It's all I can do because I couldn't help her end things the way she wanted them to end. "It's illegal," I told her. By the time she stopped talking her eyes said it all, and now even they are closed.

Diwa has fallen asleep in the armchair next to the bed. Jyoti is in the chapel consulting her God, reading her Bible, alone and isolated since I asked her to quit praying in public.

"Jesus, do you have to read that here, in front of Mother?" I said.

"Don't take the Lord's name in vain."

"It's not my lord."

"Jesus Christ is our lord and saviour."

"Please, Jyoti, would you leave it already?" I went on arguing with her at the foot of Mother's bed in clipped whispers until Diwa told us both to stop. None of us admitted that we were tired, that tired was another name for helpless, that helpless was another way to say that we'd failed her.

We are letting her die.

But no one says *dead*. Not even the nurses or doctors, and especially not me. There are other words for this; there is an entire language for dying. Euphemisms to convey the end: *departed, passed on, crossed over, deceased, at rest, at peace.* But it's not just words. It's an unspoken dialect: the tilt of the head, the watching of light and shadow in a room, the long silences, the pauses, the searching for something. The need for quiet perfection in how we circle such a finiteness that only reminds us of how poor we are at endings. How we cannot fathom conclusions in our lives. Endings are for stories and television; they are for others. Not for me and not for her.

And when the doctor did finally speak of it, he didn't proclaim it. He hesitated and lowered his head as if humbled, as if he'd failed her as well. The light in the room was low and grey blue; outside it was raining. It had been raining for days. A crow was perched on the windowsill, its back turned—all I saw was a scruff of feathers, a beak, an eye turned inward. I don't remember what

I said or what Mother said, or if either of us said anything. I think her eyes were closed. I think I looked away.

No one says *dead*.

No one talks about it, no one gives it a name or a shape, and so I talk around it, circle it, catalogue its parts, its symptoms and signs. I know it's coming but I don't know what that will mean after it arrives, or after it occurs. I don't even know if death is or if death does. Is it a noun or a verb or both? But soon I will learn that death is like a murder of crows. It darkens the sky and weighs it down. It fills my ears with a shrill cawing, a pulse and thrumming of wings, and it pushes and pulls me along the edge of the sky, leaving me teetering on the brink of this life and the next.

And then, months later, when the business of dying is over and all that must be read, divided, sold, and settled is done, it leaves me in the silence and emptiness of something never being over.

NOW

An old man in a white turban walks up and down the aisle. Each time he passes me he smiles as if he wants to say something. Across the aisle a baby sleeps in her mother's arms. Every time the plane rattles the baby wakes and the mother whispers that they are almost home.

Home.

I mouth the word and let it sit on my tongue, foreign and empty. I am going home but home feels like somewhere I can't get to anymore. It's like trying to recall a dream as it fades. Beside me Jyoti is sleeping, slumped into the empty seat that was meant for Diwa. We were stowing our bags in the car when he changed his mind. I saw it in his eyes, the way he looked out at the landscape with familiarity and longing. "I can't leave," he said.

"What do you mean?"

"I want to stay."

Jyoti paused as she opened the car door. "But our flight. It's already booked. We have to go."

"I know. I'm sorry. I just can't leave."

"But we have to."

He shook his head. "I don't have to. There's nothing waiting for me there."

"But what about us?" I said.

"Us? This place is as close to an 'us' as there has ever been."

"I don't understand." Jyoti crossed her arms over her chest. "We did what we came to do and now we have to go."

"When you go home, Nik and the children will be waiting for you. When Simran goes home, Raj and Sharon will be waiting for her. Who will be there for me?"

"We will," Jyoti said.

"You have your own families to take care of. I don't want to be a burden."

"You're not," I said.

"Even so. I want to stay." He looked out across the fields. "Something about this place feels familiar and I'm not ready to leave yet."

"Well, for how long?" I asked.

"I'm not sure."

It was quiet. The driver glanced at us, waiting for us to say stay or go. "Okay," I said.

"Okay? What do you mean, okay?" There was panic in Jyoti's voice. "You have to change his mind."

"I can't, Jyoti. It's his mind to make up."

I paused and turned to Diwa. "We'll call you when we get home."

We hugged and then stood, staring at each other, before we got in the car and drove away along the dirt road. I looked out the back window, watching Diwa get smaller and smaller until he disappeared into the landscape of grass and sky. Our lives together a series of departures.

"Sometimes you can't come home." This is what Diwa told Mother when he was thirteen. Bibi Jeet had called her to complain that Diwa wanted to cut his hair, and that when she'd asked him why he said that religion wasn't his path home. "But if you do as Bibi asks," Mother pleaded with Diwa, "maybe you can come back. Maybe Father will let you live here again."

"He won't. He never will."

A year later Bibi Jeet died and Diwa disappeared.

Even now I wonder how Diwa forgave them, or if this too was part of his forgetting. Forget the last life, forget this one too, and remember this—just this moment.

I try but I can't. Maybe it's the jet lag or the time shifts that force me to move backward and forward. Even when we land, even when I'm waiting for my luggage, watching the carousel go around, I'm lost and out of sync.

"Sim, do you mind if I go on ahead? I think Nik is waiting with the kids," Jyoti says, pulling her suitcase off the conveyer belt.

"Sure, you go on ahead." I kiss her goodbye and she rushes toward the escalators. I watch the other families, united in their fatigue, as they collect their belongings. Mine is the last suitcase to come down. When I pass through the arrival doors, Raj is the only one remaining in the waiting area.

"Sorry it took so long." I hug him for a long time, taking in the feel of his body, the smell of his cologne. I'm crying and I don't know why.

"Hey, it's okay," he says, holding me tighter. "You're home now." I nod and wipe my tears away. "Where's Diwa? I saw Jyoti, but I didn't see him."

"Long story. The short version is that he didn't want to come back just yet."

"What do you mean, just yet?"

"I don't know. At the last minute he decided he wanted to stay in India for a while."

Raj takes my suitcase and wheels it behind him as we head out of the airport. "What? Like explore his roots or something?"

"Something like that. I'll explain later."

"You must be exhausted," he says. "How long was the flight?"

"With the layover, at least twenty hours."

"Did you get any sleep on the plane?"

"You know me. I wake up almost as soon as I've fallen asleep."

We walk to the car in silence. The coastal air is light, the spring breeze wrapping itself around me. I sigh. "It's good to be home. It was so hot there, you know. It's the kind of heat that just hangs in the air and clings to you."

He says something about the mild spring before tossing my bags in the car. "Where to? Did you want me to take you to your mom's house or ours?"

"Ours."

"All right then," he says, smiling. "Sharon called, left you a message. She missed you. We both did. We both do."

"I was gone for only two weeks."

"That's not what I mean. You've been gone a long time."

"Oh." I'm realizing the weight and strain of my absence, emotional and otherwise.

"Well, I'm glad you're back." He starts the car.

When we get home I sink into a hot bath while Raj calls for takeout. "Chinese, from the place around the corner," I said when he asked what I wanted. He recites the order and then repeats himself in simple English. "Yes, two. Dinner for two." But I know that when the food arrives the order will be wrong, as it always is. I slip farther into the tub, adding more hot water until the steam rises. I run my puckered fingers over my flesh and trace the raised scar on my abdomen. Each year it fades.

"Dinner will be here in twenty minutes," Raj says, leaning into the doorway.

I nod, and just as he's turning away, I ask, "Do you ever wonder what our life might have been like if we had more children?"

He steps into the room and leans against the sink. "That's an odd question."

"Is it? I don't know." I'm avoiding his eyes.

"Do you wish we had?"

"Maybe. Sometimes it feels like someone is missing, and then I remember our baby."

"I try not to think about it." He looks at me and then away. "It was a hard time. After that I was just happy when Sharon was born healthy. Besides, we agreed that she was enough."

"She *is* enough, and for so many years I didn't think about that baby—but lately there it is. I try to push it out of my head, but it just creeps back in." I sigh, close my eyes, let the heat rise over me. "I guess with Mother gone everything feels unsettled."

"You've been through a lot."

"So have you." I run my hand through my hair, piling it on top of my head in a twist. "Having to deal with me."

"You needed time. It was probably the best thing for both of us."

"So what now?"

"I don't know. I guess we just take it day by day."

I smile. "Hand me a towel? I'm pruning up."

He watches me get out of the water and dry off. In the mirror I see his eyes linger and follow. I don't reach for a robe, I don't cover up, I let him see what the years have given and what they've taken away.

That night we make love. Moonlight filters through the open window; we are illuminated.

Afterward, loneliness and guilt settle back into my body. A distance creeps in—grief restoring herself in my chest, pressing down. Possessed, I turn away from him.

"Are you okay?" His hand on my shoulder.

"Yes and no. I don't know."

"You can talk to me."

"I know." I turn toward him and watch how the light hits his face, all angles. I trace the shapes with my fingertips. "Sometimes I just wonder how I got here. But mostly I wonder why."

He takes my hand in his. "Why what?"

"Why everything. Why Diwa went away. Why Father forgot. Why Mother died. All of it . . . And then I worry that I'm going to forget it all. That life will take over and I'll just—"

"You won't forget," he says, cutting me off. He sits up and reaches for the lamp, flooding the room in a soft light.

"But I will." I roll onto my back as if in surrender. "We're designed to forget. And when I do finally 'move on,' what will it all have meant? What's a life worth if it's so easily forgotten?"

He doesn't answer.

"Time takes away all the details. It's already reordering things. I can feel it."

"What do you mean? What does it feel like?"

I pause. I want to tell him that grief is like living in a burned-out building or a bombed city. It's like living in the aftermath of some violent end—all rubble and ruins, your body covered in a chalky film, the feeling of never being clean and good. But I don't know how to say this without alarming him and ruining whatever start we have. I get out of bed and put on my robe. Outside the streetlights are on, the road quiet with abandon. The houses are dark and full of sleep. I stare out the window, looking at ourselves reflecting back. "You know, I'm embarrassed to say that I even thought about keeping some of her ashes."

His silence invites me to finish my thought.

"That day at the river, when I was holding her in my hands and she was slipping through my fingers, I clenched my fist, trying to hang on to what little there was left."

"What changed your mind?"

"I don't know. It just seemed too awful—the idea of dividing her seemed cruel." I watch his glassy reflection, outlined in dark edges, gauging his response. He's nodding. Earnest. I turn toward him. "Did you know that you can make your dead into diamonds?"

"What?"

"Seriously, there are these companies that can extract the carbon. Through some scientific process of applying heat and pressure, ashes are transformed into diamonds."

"And you know this how?"

I sit next to him on the bed. "I stumbled on a website when I was researching funeral options . . . But it didn't seem right. Nothing did. Even scattering them, leaving her there in the water thousands of miles away, doesn't feel right."

He reaches for my hand. "You have to find a way to let go."

"You sound just like Jyoti. 'Let go. Let God.'"

"Maybe for once she's right. Letting go doesn't mean forgetting, it just means you can stop fighting it. Give in to it . . . She's gone and she's not coming back. No matter how long you think about it, you won't make sense of it."

"You're right, I know you are. It's just hard."

Raj pulls back the covers and I crawl into bed next to him as he turns out the light. Moonlight pours in through the sheer draperies, shadows scattering across the walls, and for a moment the world feels as if it exists just for me. I drift in and out of a quiet that's not a real quiet but an unquiet, the sound of God waiting for me to notice him. I resist the urge to pray.

In the morning, I leave the house before dawn. Raj is asleep, his arm extended to where I lay beside him. I kiss his cheek and tell him that I'll be home soon. "There's something I need to do." He nods, eyes closed and full of dreams.

Mother's house is quiet and cold. The furnace hasn't been on since we left; it seems as though the chill has embedded itself in the walls. I reach into the closet, put on her favourite cardigan, and then head into the backyard. The tulips have peaked and are wilted now, their downturned stalks and scattered petals making way for summer's long arm. I kneel beside them and push my hands into the soil. Beneath the first layer of earth, the ground is still packed. I get up again and walk to the shed in search of her garden tools. As I rummage through them I hear her voice in my head telling me that it's time.

"Time for what?" I ask.

No answer. It wasn't her voice. It was mine.

In the garden, I dig until I hear the trowel strike glass. I reach inside the hole, unearthing the poem jar. Then I sit down cross-legged in the dirt, unscrew the lid, and empty the contents in my lap. The slips are worn through, tattered, the writing faded. Except for a few. I lay them side by side and order them into a haiku, counting syllables.

> *And when we were young*
> *Love was a burning map of*
> *Forgetting ourselves.*

I read it over and over, committing it to memory before putting the slips back in the jar. Then I take a matchbook out of my pocket and strike one, watching the flame flicker before tossing it in. The poems ignite, curl into themselves, a slow burn.

ACKNOWLEDGMENTS

Satvinder, Amit, and Arun, for being my now, then, and before. My sister Kulbinder for being my first reader and for being so open with her thoughts and ideas. To all of my sisters, for constantly inspiring me with their wisdom and care. My mother and father, their lives are an example of everything that matters. My agent, John Pearce, for his patience, faith, and feedback. My publishers at Penguin Random House Canada and HarperCollins US for their enthusiasm. My editors, Shima Aoki and Sofia Groopman, for their collaborative insights and editorial comments that were thought-provoking and forward-looking. Alissa York for her fine advice and critical feedback that pushed the novel into new directions. Coleman Barks for his permission to include select Rumi translations from which I drew inspiration. Rumi, Rabindranath Tagore, Kahlil Gibran, Jiddu Krishnamurti, and the many great poets and thought leaders whose work is transformational. The Royal College of Psychiatrists for granting me permission to use the Edinburgh Postnatal Depression Scale. The Sage Hill Writing Experience for providing me with dedicated time and space for writing. The Canada Council for the Arts for their support of this project. My friends and family for being a lifeline and for our many lifetimes.